DEATHMAN, DO NOT FOLLOW ME

JAY BENNETT

SCHOLASTIC INC.
New York Toronto London Auckland Sydney

ISBN 0-590-44006-3

Copyright © 1968 by Jay Bennett. All rights reserved. Published by Scholastic Inc., 730 Broadway, New York, NY 10003, by arrangement with E.P. Dutton, Inc. POINT is a registered trademark of Scholastic Inc.

12 11 10 9 8 7 6 5 4 3 2 1   0 1 2 3/9

Printed in the U.S.A.   01

For Dad and Mother

PART ONE

DISCOVERY

1

We walk along and everything is fine. Just fine. The sun is shining, and the street is full of laughter and the sound of merry voices. We are young and happy and glad to be alive. We walk along, and suddenly everything is no longer fine. Something has swept away the laughter and the voices. Something, like a great hand, has drawn down the night. And we begin to know fear.

Danny Morgan sat in the large, crowded schoolroom and listened to the drone of the teacher's voice. He longed for the end of the session and release. This was the last class of a long day, and Danny was eager to get outside while there was still light.

Every day with the closing bell of school, Danny would cross Flatbush Avenue and then make his way through the busy Brooklyn streets to Prospect Park. Then he would walk through the park on his way home. He liked walking alone through the park on his way home. He liked walking alone through the quiet trees while the wind rustled softly. It brought up warm, pleasant thoughts. Thoughts of summers in upstate New York. Memories of the slap of water against the wet wood of a rowboat. The sight of black crows soaring high over the sparkling lake, their dark hard bodies piercing the sky and then fading over the slim tops of trees. Fading, fading . . . till the lake was silent and alone again.

"Morgan."

Danny suddenly realized that the teacher, Mr. Warfield, was speaking to him.

"Yes?" Danny heard himself say. His voice seemed distant and strange.

"Morgan, would you please rise while I'm talking to you?"

Danny slowly rose, a flush spreading over his face.

"I'm sorry, sir," Danny said.

Mr. Warfield smiled. He liked the tall, lean boy with the quiet eyes and rangy body.

"Could you tell me a bit about the life of Van Gogh?" Mr. Warfield asked.

"Van Gogh?"

There was a puzzled look on Danny's face. He ran his hand through his dark hair and then let it fall to his side.

"His feverish but productive days at Arles."

"Arles?"

"Van Gogh and Gauguin."

"Gauguin?"

"And Van Gogh. I've just finished speaking about him, Morgan. I thought I spoke with interest and feeling. Evidently I didn't."

The smile was gone from Mr. Warfield's face. "Haven't you been listening?"

Danny didn't speak. He felt angry with himself for not listening. The least he could've done was to listen. True, he didn't care too much about art, and though he liked Mr. Warfield as a man, he didn't care too much for him as a teacher. Danny had definite ideas about teaching. He hoped someday to be a teacher. After he had played a few years of professional football.

Daniel Thomas Morgan had his life all planned out for himself. One more year of high school football, four years of college football at U.C. L.A., and then three or four seasons with the New York Giants or the Los Angeles Rams. Then he would settle down to teaching in a small college in upstate New York. Near the lake with the dark crows flying high over the sparkling water.

"You're dreaming again, Morgan," Mr. Warfield said.

Danny flushed.

"I've been waiting rather patiently for you to tell me about that great Dutch painter who did much to influence modern art. I've been waiting."

He paused and repeated in clipped accents: "Rather patiently."

Danny heard some desperate but vague whisperings spring up behind him. Some of his classmates were trying to help him. But he couldn't make out clearly what they were saying. He thought he heard the words "Brooklyn Museum," but he wasn't sure. He strained to hear better, and as he did he felt a sudden bitterness against himself and Mr. Warfield. A bitterness which led to a fierce impulse to turn and walk out of the classroom, to go clattering down the wide steps and out of the huge, gray stone building, along the busy streets, to the quiet, soothing comfort of the park.

But Danny stood there. The whispering became more urgent and more clear. Danny heard the word "exhibit."

"Cut that out," Mr. Warfield said to the class. "If you want to help him, then speak up." His voice rang out like an army sergeant's, trailing out the words. "Loud and clear." He said it again, this time rolling the *r* vigorously:

"Loud and clear."

The whispering abruptly stopped. A silence rushed in, and Danny was alone again.

"Well?"

Mr. Warfield's small gray eyes were concentrated fully upon the tall youth. He was a solid, stocky man with strong brown hair that was beginning to show glints of gray. His face was rugged and leathery, the face of a man who had lived much in the hard open air. The lines about his mouth were deep and long, like two dark slashes.

"I'm waiting, Morgan."

For a moment Danny tried to think back to the movie he had seen more than a year ago. The one with Kirk Douglas as Vincent Van Gogh. But the night he had seen it was the night before the big game with Erasmus Hall High School. Danny hadn't paid too much attention to Kirk Douglas. He had been too busy going over in his mind the important plays for the next day. Now he wished he had forgotten the game and concentrated upon Kirk Douglas. They had lost the game anyway — by a big and humiliating score.

Danny decided to make a stab at it.

"Vincent Van Gogh was an artist," he said and instantly realized the utter absurdity of what he was saying. He repeated in a low voice, "An artist."

"Wonderful," Mr. Warfield said with tight lips.

His speech was now precise. Very precise. It did not seem to go with the rugged, angular face.

"You've made a truly wonderful start." He turned his attention to the class but still spoke to Danny. "I thought you were going to say he was a quarterback for the Minnesota Vikings."

Danny's face became red as the class laughed. For an instant he looked fiercely at the teacher. Their eyes locked. Then Mr. Warfield said quietly:

"I've been telling the class about the new Van Gogh that's being shown at the Brooklyn Mu-

9

seum. It has never been seen before in this country. The painting is attracting thousands from all over the city."

Mr. Warfield paused. When he began again, his voice was biting.

"Why is the painting attracting thousands from all over the city, Mr. Quarterback?"

"I wish you wouldn't call me that," Danny said.

The two looked squarely at each other. A heavy silence hung over the crowded classroom. The long thin rays of the winter sun came through the high windows and fell upon the two figures, lighting their faces and casting the rest of their bodies into shadow.

Mr. Warfield nodded.

"You are right," he said slowly. "The season is over now. You are no longer a quarterback."

"The season is over, Mr. Warfield."

Mr. Warfield nodded again.

"But tell me. Is it ever over for you? Aren't you still playing your football?"

"No."

"On imaginary gridirons?"

Danny didn't speak.

"The gridirons of your empty mind?"

Danny was about to retort, but the shrill ring of the school bell cut between them. Mr. Warfield motioned curtly to the silent class.

"You can all go."

Then he turned to Danny and said:

"You can stay."

After the class was gone, Danny sat and looked

through the window at the darkening sky. Mr. Warfield sat at his desk and busied himself with some school records. A fly came through the open doorway, buzzed through the empty room, circled and circled again, and then settled down on one of the silent desks. Danny gloomily watched it sharpen its two legs, one against the other. The tiny wings fluttered rapidly, iridescent in the half-light. Danny watched them till they stopped. The iridescence vanished. Danny stopped watching.

The fly finally buzzed up from the desk and out of the room. It has freedom, Danny thought. It comes and goes as it wants to. Soon it will find an open window and fly out into the air and away down the evening sky. Like a tiny bird set free.

Danny remembered how his father used to tell him stories about birds, all sorts of birds, just before he went to bed. That was years ago. So many, many years ago. Like it happened in the ice age. He wondered why certain images stay with you.

He turned gloomily away from the open doorway and looked through the high window at the dying day.

"What the hell's with you?" the teacher suddenly snapped.

Danny stared at him, down along the aisle of empty desks.

"I say again, what the hell's with you?" Mr. Warfield said harshly. His voice seemed to rap against the walls.

Danny was silent.

"Does my language startle you?"

The teacher's face was set hard. He had shoved aside the record book, suddenly, violently, as though he had suddenly become aware of Danny and the sight of the youth had angered him.

"Does it? Hell is a bad word for a teacher to use to a student. Isn't it?"

Mr. Warfield's right hand hit the top of his desk for emphasis. Danny noticed a long, jagged scar running near the knuckles. He had never noticed it before. But now looking at its whitened edges he remembered hearing that the teacher had been a Japanese prisoner in the last war. He had survived the Bataan Death March.

"A bad word. But it's the only way to talk to you. To stir you up. Do you think I like to humiliate you before a class? But do you give me any choice?"

Danny was still silent.

"Why are you such a loner? Why is it so hard to reach you? You frustrate a person. Do you hear me? You make a man want to tear his hair out. Is there anything wrong at home?"

"No," Danny finally said.

"You're happy there?"

"Happy?"

The teacher spread his hands wide.

"Nobody's completely happy anywhere. Do you feel comfortable there?"

"Yes," Danny said.

He didn't like this line of questioning, but he knew he had to answer. There was no way out.

"What does your father think of you?"

"My father?"

"How does he get along with you? How do you get along with him? Take your time and tell me something about your relationship. Are you pals? Are you strangers? Do you just live together and tolerate each other?"

"I have no father," Danny said. "He's dead."

He said it simply, without any emotion.

"Recently? Or a long time ago?"

"A long time," Danny said.

Sometimes it feels like it happened yesterday. Like he was just standing there. And then he was gone.

"Your mother work?"

Danny nodded. When the teacher spoke again, his voice was gentle.

"It's good to dream. But it's better to make yourself a part of a life about you. Believe me. There's no percentage the other way. I know."

He looked at Danny and then said again, "I know."

Danny was about to ask Mr. Warfield how he knew, but the words did not come.

"Have you friends?"

"Yes."

"Fellows?"

"Yes."

"Girls?"

"Yes."

"Any special girl?"

Danny didn't answer.

"You can tell me it's none of my business," Mr. Warfield said.

"It's none of your business," Danny said quietly.

A smile flitted across the teacher's face and then was gone. Danny felt the smile warm him, and for an instant he felt close to the man. But the resentment at being kept in after school pushed the feeling away. Because of him he was missing walking through the park while the sun was still out.

"You have friends, and yet you're a loner," Mr. Warfield said, breaking the silence that had come between them.

"Maybe."

"Maybe," Mr. Warfield echoed a bit grimly.

He got up and paced his side of the room. Danny kept to his seat at the other end of the long room.

"You're a strange kid. You go out for a sport. You make good at it. And yet you're always alone. Even when you're a vital part of a team."

Danny wondered how Mr. Warfield knew.

"That's the way I am," Danny said.

"Why?"

"It's the way I am."

"Again I ask you, why?"

"I don't know," Danny said stubbornly.

Mr. Warfield had stopped his pacing. He stood there, his thick shadow thrust against the wall and almost reaching to the blackboard.

"Any brothers?"

Danny shook his head.

"Sisters?"

Danny shook his head again.

"You live in an apartment or a private house?"

"An apartment."

"How many rooms?"

14

"Four."

"You have a room for yourself?"

"Yes."

"What kind of a block do you live on?"

"What kind?"

"Is it noisy? Quiet? Trees?"

"It's quiet, and it has trees," Danny said, and there was a bit of pride in his voice. He liked the block very much.

"Where is it?"

"Troop Place."

The thick shadow wavered along the high wall and stopped. Outside on the streets the lights had switched on. But the darkness had not yet fully come.

"Troop Place? I never heard of it."

"Not many people have heard of it," Danny explained. "Even people who've lived in Brooklyn all their lives. It's a small street on the other side of Prospect Park. Quiet and small."

"Evidently you like it there."

"Yes."

"Any friends on the block?"

"A few."

"You keep to yourself most of the time, don't you?"

He broke a piece of chalk, and the white dust puffed up, gleaming in the dimness of the room.

"Keep to yourself. You like it best that way. Alone on that quiet and small block that's out of the way. Like a backwater village high in some hills. Away from everything. So far, far away. It's your cave. Your foxhole."

15

Danny didn't speak.

Mr. Warfield went back to his chair and sat down slowly. He sighed and then drummed his thick fingers on the top of the desk. A steady, rhythmic beat. He wasn't even looking at Danny anymore. His eyes had a sad, faraway look in them.

"You trouble me, Morgan. Greatly."

Danny wondered why Mr. Warfield always gave him more attention than anybody else in the entire class. It often puzzled him. It had been that way from the very first day of the term.

Mr. Warfield was now looking down at the jagged scar on his right hand.

"Tomorrow is Saturday. I want you to go to that exhibit."

"At the Brooklyn Museum?"

"The Van Gogh."

Danny rose.

"Can I leave now, Mr. Warfield?"

The teacher looked up and nodded. Danny started slowly for the doorway.

"I'll expect a thorough, first-class report from you Monday," Mr. Warfield said firmly.

Danny nodded and went out of the room.

2

He was walking along, slowly, thoughtfully, thinking of Mr. Warfield, when as if from a great distance he heard someone call his name. As if from a great and shimmering distance.

Danny turned and waited. While he waited, he still thought of Mr. Warfield and the hand with the jagged scar. Somehow, for some reason, somewhere way deep inside of him, the scar had frightened him. He couldn't figure out why. He just couldn't. Then he forgot the hand and the scar and Mr. Warfield.

The voice was now upon him. Friendly and familiar. The voice of his schoolmate, George Cheever.

"Hello, Danny."

"Hello, George."

"Mind if I walk you through the park?"

"Come along."

They crossed the busy street and then went through the high stone arch, gray in the twilight, and into the park. The noise of Flatbush Avenue dimmed behind them and then died out completely. Danny felt his gloom and resentment slowly leave him. A lightening peace drifted into his being. He felt good.

"Care for a cigarette?" George asked.

"No."

"I don't either," George said, putting the pack back into his coat pocket. "I don't know why I smoke. Do you know why we smoke?"

He had a pleasant, easy voice. Danny liked listening to George Cheever speak. He sometimes wished that George could come up with him to the lake in the summertime and sit in the sun and just talk in his pleasant easy voice. Just talk the hours away. About nothing. Simply nothing. Like, why do we smoke?

"Do you know why we smoke?" George asked again.

"Because men do."

Danny had never thought of the matter, but now that he did the answer came quickly. As if it had been there all the time waiting for expression.

Because men do.

He wondered, now that he had said it, how many things fellows like him do that men do. Just because men do them. Just because of that and no other reason at all.

"No reason at all," he murmured, echoing the thought within.

George had finished pondering Danny's answer.

"But we're athletes. Football players. It's no damn good for our wind. You know how you

feel when the fourth quarter comes rou
your legs start to give out on you."

"You never smoke in season."

"True."

They were silent. Then George suddenly stopped before a darkening oak and asked:

"So why should I smoke out of season? An athlete should keep in condition all the time. All the time, man."

He clapped his hands for emphasis. The sound echoed like a shot into the dying evening.

"Stop smoking."

"So why don't I?"

"I don't know."

"So why don't I?" George repeated. "I got it all figured out like a math equation. Cigarettes equal cancer equals death. Yet I go ahead and buy me a pack of cigarettes. Spend forty-three cents that could go to my daddy's lunch. My mom always says that. No end to her saying that. Like a song."

"He works hard for his money," Danny said, and as the words fell away into the silence, he thought of the tall blond man, his own father, the tall blond man with the quiet blue eyes and the slow walk. The man who was a mailman and lugged a mail sack summer and winter and had always wanted to be a lawyer and had ended up being nothing but a memory.

"He worked hard for his money," Danny heard himself say, while his eyes misted up for an instant, just for an instant and no more.

"He sure does," George agreed. "I shouldn't

take that money from him. Not for cigarettes, I shouldn't. Here he comes home, cement dust still on him and his eyes all tired out, and I — I —" He shook his head. "Just don't make sense, Danny. Don't make sense."

They walked along quietly. A slight wind had come up and was rustling the waters of the darkening lake. High in the sky, the first stars were out, the very first ones, glistening and wavering. A hush was over the vast park.

"Soon be winter," George said.

"It will," Danny nodded.

Danny thought of the expense of a new overcoat and didn't say anything. He would try to get through this winter with his old one but he was sure his mother wouldn't like it. Even though they needed the money, she wouldn't like it.

"Feel it in my bones," George said.

They walked along silently. They had known each other from elementary school days. Now they were in high school together. Soon they would be out of high school — before they knew it. And then maybe they would break up and go their separate ways. That's what life does at times. It comes in and breaks people apart. Takes them and blows them apart like leaves in a big wind. Sometimes blowing them away for good and forever.

Like it did to me and my father. Before I even got to know him, he was gone. Time sometimes goes too fast, Danny thought. Much, much too fast. They say the young want to grow up fast. But it's the old who say that.

"Snow and ice," George said. "Plenty of it."
The old.

Sometimes the old should just leave us alone, Danny thought grimly. Let us figure out things for ourselves. Maybe we would come up with a world that would make sense. It's sure as hell theirs doesn't.

"Can feel it in the sky," George said. "A long, cold winter."

Their footsteps struck the pavement with a sharp and steady rhythm. Danny Morgan was taller than George Cheever; George was the wider and thicker figured of the two. Every time they passed under the sweep of lamplight, Danny's white skin gleamed while George's dark brown face shone like copper.

Their footsteps rapped along the hard stone of the pavement, striking off sounds the way sparks are struck off from cold flint. Danny kept listening to the rhythmic sounds and kept thinking of Mr. Warfield's harsh and cutting words.

"Loner."

Harsh and cutting words.

"Loner. You're a loner."

"What are you thinking of?" George asked.

"Nothing," Danny answered.

"You looked like you were thinking of something. Something that hurt."

They walked over a path they knew down through the years. Many times Danny had walked it alone, many times with George. Under one arm they carried their books, tight and snug, the other arm swung free. After a while they paused by an old, paint-peeled wooden bench and sat down, first one and then the other. Their shoulders touched while they sat in complete silence. A breeze blew up and ruffled their hair and then quieted down. The air was still again.

"No more school till Monday." George sighed in relief.

The light from the overhead lamp sprayed through the dead branches of a huge maple tree and down upon the two figures. The lean, tall one and the wide, muscular one. Two figures, close and yet apart.

Out on the lake, in the last part of the sky that was not yet black, the sun had crashed in a burst of reds and violets. The water stirred with violence and beauty.

"Look at it," George said. "Just look at it."

"Yes," Danny whispered.

They sat watching the quivering lake. A poignancy had come into Danny's dark eyes. George's deep brown eyes shone.

"I could paint it," George said wistfully. "I sure wish I could paint it."

"Why don't you try?" Danny said gently.

"Maybe I will. Maybe I'll go out and get me some oils and paintbrushes and some canvases, and come back here and just sit down and do it. Just do a sunset." His voice rose and rang out over the lake. "And I'd call it: 'Sunset on the Lake in Prospect Park Just Before Winter Came and Covered the Water with Ice.'"

He laughed at Danny, a wide and pleasant laugh.

"How do you like that for a title? The Rolling Stones could make a song out of it. A real blast."

He beat his hand on the bench in a rock beat and hummed and then laughed again.

"A real blast."

Danny kept looking out at the fierce night rushing in and slamming away the beauty, and he didn't say anything.

"Maybe I will," George said after a pause. "Maybe I'll just get up the spirit and the energy and just do it. Maybe I will. Someday."

"Someday never comes," Danny said, and a bitterness had crept back into his being.

"Maybe it will come," George said doggedly.

Danny glanced at his friend's face. The light tracing the straight, even features gave them a clean line. The brown, squarish chin seemed resolute. The full lips firm. Danny turned and looked toward the lake. It was now dark. Completely dark.

Within him was the same pervading darkness. Pervading and unrelieved.

Loner. Loner. Even when you have a friend you are a loner. Even then. Yes, Mr. Daniel Thomas Morgan. Yes.

Then he felt George's hand on his shoulder for a fleeting instant, and he heard him say:

"That Warfield man gave you a hard time."

Danny shrugged and kicked a little stone that lay on the ground before him. It clattered away into the silence.

"A real hard time, Danny."

"Maybe I had it coming to me," Danny said.

"In front of the whole class? Like you're a clown on a stage?"

"I had it coming."

George shook his head vehemently.

"Not for not knowing about Van Gogh. So what about Van Gogh? So what?"

"I wasn't listening."

"So you don't listen. Millions of people don't listen. They stand on street corners and talk to each other and don't listen to a word. Not a single mumbling word." He pounded on the bench wood for emphasis. "Truth? Answer me. Truth or not truth?"

Then he lifted his hands expressively and snorted out:

"So you don't listen. What a bunch of garbage."

Danny didn't say anything. He sat looking straight ahead of him, his lean face tight with feeling and thought.

"Garbage," George repeated with force and was silent.

A policeman came by, his shadow sweeping obliquely across the ground and toward the lake, like a falling giant. He glanced at the two and went on. The sound of his footsteps slowly dimmed away.

"A real hard time," George murmured angrily. "I felt like saying something to him."

Danny turned sharply to George. His eyes flashed.

"Stay out of it. It's between him and me."

"Sure, Danny. Sure." George said soothingly.

Danny had risen and was about to go off,

leaving George sitting there, but he slowly sat down again.

"Just stay out of it," Danny said, and this time his voice was gentle, for he had seen the hurt come to his friend's face.

"You're calling the signals." George smiled while the hurt slowly faded out of the deep-brown eyes. "Calling the signals. Like you do on the football field. And we guys listen."

Danny rested his hand on George's thick shoulder.

Somewhere deep in the distance the sound of a dog began, a deep and baying sound. It floated across the wide expanse of the lake into them. Then it stopped.

"Sometimes I call pretty bad signals," Danny said, smiling ruefully.

"Sometimes you do," George grinned. "Like in the Monroe game. That sure was a bad call."

"It was."

"Three yards from the goal line, and you call a pass play. Just three little yards.

"A bad call." Danny suddenly laughed and wondered how he could laugh now when then it had been a disaster. Sheer, overwhelming disaster. He hadn't been able to sleep for days after that game.

He laughed again, feeling free as he laughed, as if a weight had been lifted from him.

"You admit it now," George chuckled.

"A bad call." Danny nodded. "Couldn't have been worse."

"Listen to him. Just listen to him finally admit it."

"Better late than never."

"Right."

George laughed and ducked his shoulder into Danny as if to block him out of a play. Danny laughed and feinted away from him and got up from the bench. He felt a sudden exhilaration.

"Come on," he challenged. "I'll race you out of the park. Race you for a quarter to Troop Place."

"You're on."

"Show your money."

"Show yours."

They held up quarters to the lamplight, and the silver coins shone and sparkled and almost laughed aloud.

"Take your ten-yard handicap," Danny said.

"How about fifteen this time?"

"What?"

"You beat me with ten last time. Fair is fair."

"Fifteen?"

"Uh-huh."

"Don't know if I could do it."

"You're like the wind, Danny."

"Stop conning me."

"Fifteen. Come on."

Danny weighed it for a moment and came to a decision.

"Okay. Pace it off."

"Honest and square."

George moved out of the circle of light, measuring off slowly and very exactly the fifteen yards. Each step drew him farther and farther into the surrounding darkness.

"Fifteen," George finally called.

"Fifteen?"

"That's what it is."

"Sounds like fifty."

"You heard me count it off."

"I heard," Danny muttered.

Danny could no longer make out George's figure. All he was aware of was a voice, a disembodied voice. The night seemed to have suddenly become blacker. He felt a strange sensing of tragedy and disaster. He couldn't understand why he felt it. He had never feared the darkness before. In fact he had always welcomed it.

"Ready," Danny shouted.

"Ready," he heard.

"Get set," Danny shouted.

"Set," he heard.

The voice seemed to float in as if it were on a mist.

"Go!"

"Goooooooooo!"

He ran after the departing voice, and as he did, he thought he saw out of the corner of his eye, standing against a row of bare-branched trees, just where the light stopped and the darkness began, the figure of Mr. Warfield.

He knew he was wrong. That nobody was there.

Yet it made Danny run through the black night even faster.

3

As he sat in his room doing his history homework
that night, he thought of the race and his first
burst of terror — and the feeling of tragedy and
and disaster.

The race was lost. Even though he ran like the
wind, a huge hand pushing at his back, George
ran even faster. Every time he got close, George
put on a burst of speed and pulled away. At the
end they both were winded and spent. George
went off jingling the quarters in his hand, carry-
ing the silver sounds deep into the night.

Till they were lost.

Only the memory of the race now remained. Only
that and the figure of Mr. Warfield standing
against a row of bare-branched trees in a black
night.

"Danny."

Danny turned from the little desk he used and
looked questioningly at his mother. She had just
come into his room.

"Am I disturbing you?"

"No, Mom."

She was a tall woman, tall like his father. Tall and quiet like he had been. Danny often wondered how two people so alike could be married to each other. They both came from Brooklyn, yet they had the quietness and taciturnity of Maine people — just like some of the farm people he knew upstate in the summertime.

He had rarely heard them quarrel. For that matter, they rarely raised their voices. At one time he had resented it terribly. At one time he had felt it was wrong. Terribly, terribly wrong. A fellow should hear raised voices in his house. Just as he heard sometimes when he was visiting friends. In George Cheever's flat the voices were always raised. There was a lot of laughing going on there. And there was some anger. There were tears. George's father yelled hard and loud, and when the yelling was over and the walls stopped shaking, he would grab George tight and run his hand through his hair.

Here was always quietness, even before his father died. It was always there. He had resented it. But finally he got used to it. He shrugged his shoulders and said to himself, with the same quietness that was all about him, "People are people."

He said it on the day he came running home from school, a medal hot in his grip, his breath short, eyes eager for the faces of his mother and his father. He rang the apartment bell again and again just for the joy of it even though he had the apartment key in his pocket. Rang it and rang it. When the door swung open, he held the medal high, the gold, shining medal.

They had stood looking at him, their faces slowly taking on the shine of the medal. As they closed the door behind him, they laughed softly and were proud of him, very proud. His mother murmured, "Danny, Danny," over and over again, while his father patted his back tenderly, very tenderly. Then they put the medal on the living room mantel so that all who came in might see. He could feel the whole apartment shining with a mute joy.

But it was then, then, that he wanted raised voices and great laughter. Even a shout of anger that would shake the walls would have been better. Even that would have been better, Danny thought to himself, looking at the tall, almost lithe figure of his mother.

"You're sure I'm not disturbing you, Danny?"

She stood there near the doorway, a dark-haired, small-featured woman with quiet, gray eyes. The dim, soft light of the hall fell on part of her face, tracing a gleam onto her lips and bringing a glow to her eyes and hair. But as she came farther into the room and away from the soft light, he saw with a pang that her beauty was fading from her. There was a tiredness to the gray, quiet eyes, and a slackness had almost set in at the mouth. For an instant he thought of the lake at sunset, the violets and the reds streaking the sky and water, the lake in beautiful, quivering sunset — and then the blackness rushing in and slamming it out.

"Your face looked so sad, Danny. What is it?"

"Nothing, Mom."

His father had once told him how beautiful she was. They were sitting watching a bird fly — a sleek, iridescent bird winging into the sunlight.

"Are you sure, Danny?"

She stood poised and concerned.

"I'm sure, Mom," he said, his eyes still on her.

Then he smiled gently and motioned her to the old easy chair that stood next to his dresser. She sat down slowly, almost hesitantly, just as the girls in his class did when they came in late and Mr. Warfield had already begun the lesson. Slowly, hesitantly, yet so gracefully.

Danny turned his desk chair about and now faced her.

"Go ahead," he said.

But he knew that she wouldn't. She glanced about the room at the narrow maple bed, the bookcases flanking it, filled with textbooks, novels, and some issues of the *National Geographic* stacked next to issues of *Playboy*. The gold football that stood center bureau, the blue-and-red school pennants that hung on the wall behind it. Her eyes paused on a large photograph of Bob Dylan.

"Any new records?" she asked.

"No."

"I saw a picture biography of him in Brentano's. Just came out a few days ago."

"George Cheever was telling me about it. Maybe we'll chip in and buy it together. If we can see our way clear."

"Seems to be an interesting book. I glanced through it. Some excellent photographs."

"Dylan's an interesting guy."

"He is."

They were silent.

"He's a loner," Danny suddenly said and didn't know why he said it to her.

"Dylan?"

"Yes."

"Why do you say that?"

"I don't know."

"Some of his songs are lonely," she said. "But I don't think he is."

"He's a loner," Danny said.

"Do you know much of his life?"

"Enough."

Their voices were low, and he found himself remembering again that the voices were always low in this house.

"How is George Cheever these days?" she asked, after a pause.

"Okay."

"Weren't you both on a science project?"

"Science project?"

"Awhile back."

He remembered and nodded, but he was still thinking about Dylan and loneliness.

"How did it come out?"

"Pretty good."

"How good?"

She never asked him about schoolwork. She always waited patiently for him to tell her.

"Doctor Johnson seemed to like it pretty much," he said.

"Doctor Johnson?"

"He's head of the department. The physics department."

Her face lighted up, and he saw the tired lines leave her eyes for a moment. But he knew they would be back. The tiny tired lines would be back to steal her beauty from her. One day they would steal it from her for good. He would look at her and see that she had become old.

"How much did he like it?"

"Oh. Thought it was the best he had seen in a long while."

"Really?"

"Uh-huh."

She smiled proudly at him. She looked away from him. Then she turned back to him and said hesitantly:

"It has to do with magneto-hydro — ?" She stopped and laughed softly, and then said almost shyly, "When it comes to modern science, I'm an illiterate."

"You do okay."

"An illiterate."

He knew that she wanted to get it right, so she could tell her colleagues at the Montague Street library all about it. He remembered that, when his father was alive, she rarely spoke of her son's accomplishments to her fellow librarians. Only if questioned would she talk about him and then reticently. They both were that way. They carried their pride and their important feelings deep within them. But now she seemed to open up more and more when it came to him. He noticed it, and he thought about it.

"It's magneto-hydrodynamics," he said. "A big name that doesn't mean much."

She said the long word slowly, very slowly. Enjoying it, as if he had created it new and given it to the world of science.

"Magneto-hydrodynamics."

"There," he smiled. "You got it first try."

"Sounds awfully imposing."

"They all do these days. Big names, but they don't mean much."

"I'm sure they do, Danny."

He shook his head.

"The same as in football, Mom. Lots of big names for lots of old, simple plays. Fancy sportswriter names. The T formation has become the superdooper, lalapala. . . ."

He stopped and shrugged and smiled at her blank face. He had lost her. He knew that she never had and never would understand football. It was a mystery to her. But she had come to every game that he ever played in. Come and sat and watched from the opening soaring kick to the last final gunshot. He never could make out what went on in her mind while she sat there and watched and rose with the crowd at the exciting moments. He remembered once looking up from the huddle and searching for her in the crowd and seeing her and wondering. It was a mystery to him that he knew he would never solve.

"It's the age of advertising creeping in everywhere," he said. "Even into science. Superhextroclorodyne. No toothpaste is good without superhextroclorodyne, Mom. You know that." His eyes were smiling as he spoke, but his voice had become edged with a fine bitterness. "The age of advertising."

He was about to add, it's the age of the phony, of the liar, of the old trying to pull a fast one on the young, but he knew it would hurt her to hear him say that. So he cut the words off.

Instead he said:

"I'll work up a short summary of the project for you if you want."

"I would, Danny. Very much."

"Simple language."

"Very."

"Okay," he said gently.

She looked thankfully at him. Then she said:

"When you see George Cheever, give him my congratulations."

"I will."

They were silent. She had come to ask him something, and he waited patiently for her to do it. Danny wondered what was troubling her. He noticed that as he grew older his mother grew more dependent on him. She was making him more and more the head of the house. He felt that she was proud and sad, heartbreakingly sad that this should be happening.

In a way he welcomed her dependence on him, and in a way he feared it. He felt it was making him grow up too fast, much too fast.

She glanced at the old record player that stood

in the corner of the room. The records were stacked on a wooden shelf above the player, in a long and silent row. She seemed to be counting them, record by record. Aimlessly counting them, yet her small, oval face was quiet and absorbed.

A car stopped outside the house, and the sound came up to them. A metal door opened and slammed shut. A voice lifted, held, then wavered, and vanished into the night. The car went off. Troop Place was silent again.

"The Carsons feel you play your records a bit too loudly, Danny," she suddenly said.

But he knew that this was not why she had come into his room.

"That's the way they should be played," he said quietly. "Loudly."

She had turned away from the record player and was now looking at him.

"Perhaps you could tone it down a bit. Just a bit, Danny."

"They're never home. What are they complaining about?"

"I know, Danny. But let's appease them."

"I don't believe in appeasement, Mom. Look what happened to the world when Chamberlain appeased Hitler."

He had been writing about that era when she came into his room. Nineteen thirty-eight and Munich were fresh and alive to him. It made him bitter to read of the hawk-faced man with the umbrella swung high overhead selling out a world. In the essay he was writing he had chosen words that were cutting and damning. It was the case of the old selling out the young, he had written. Who got killed in the war that followed? Who but the young? Who but the young always pay for the mistakes and cruelties of the old?

He was going to end the essay with these words: Why do you always put war into us when there is no war in us? When there is peace and love in us and the dream of a sun over a summer lake?

Why?

He was going to end the essay with one word in large capital letters:

WHY?

But she had come in and stopped him before he could put those sentences down. Stopped him without even knowing what he was writing. She had come in, and he had put his pen down.

"The Carsons are not Hitlers, Danny," she said almost severely.

"They're not," he admitted.

"They're decent people."

"They are."

"They have their rights."

"They do," he said, and now there was a twinkle in his eyes. He knew how his mother loved to be at peace with her neighbors, and the Carsons were neighbors. Right over their heads.

"You'll lower it then?"

"I'll lower it," he said.

She leaned back in the easy chair and was silent again. He waited for her to speak.

The shade of the front window began to flap.

Danny got up and went to the window and closed it. As he did, he caught a glimpse of the distant trees of the park, their bare branches outlined against a burst of stars. Beyond the stars was a patch of blackness.

The shade fell back against the window, blocking out the trees, the stars, the blackness.

"Danny."

He turned to her.

"Danny, I stopped off at the drugstore on the way home. Mr. Dorman tells me you want to work for him."

"That's right," Danny said, but within him was a dull anger at the druggist for speaking. They had agreed that nothing was to be said until Danny had been working there awhile.

Now it was all lost.

"I wish you wouldn't, Danny."

"It'll be a few hours every night and all day Saturday. I'll have enough time for study," he said patiently.

She leaned forward to him, and her voice was earnest.

"But there's no need for it, Danny."

"There is."

"I make enough for the two of us."

"Do you?"

"Yes."

He shook his head.

"No, Mom."

"We manage. We manage quite well."

"I'll need an overcoat."

"I'll buy it for you."

"I'd like to buy it with my own money."

"No."

"Mom, I want to work. I don't work all through the football season. I don't feel right about it."

"I said we manage."

He felt he was pushing against her thought. Pushing against it and making no headway. It made him fumble for speech. He found emotion still held tight with him, still fiercely controlled, yet blocking and tangling his words, making them hard to come out the way he wanted them to. Even his voice seemed strange to him.

"I — I don't know how to say it to you. But it — it's false pride — or — or something. I — I just — I — "

His words trailed off into silence.

"False pride?"

"I — I don't know."

"False pride? Is that what you're saying? A matter of pride?"

It was the way she said it that opened him up. He felt that she was lying to herself. That she knew it was false pride, and yet she was lying to herself. And to him.

This time his words suddenly loosed themselves and came out sharp and even.

"If you need money, then it's no shame for your son to go out and work for it. No shame at all."

"That's enough, Danny. You've said enough."

"Have I?"

"Danny."

She had risen, and he could now see how upset she was over the matter. He felt a flash of pity for her. But he still found it hard to control his anger. His anger at the injustice of the whole damned thing. Other parents nag their sons to work. Get on their backs and never get off till they do work. And here she . . . she . . . Damn it. Damn it!

But he turned away from her, went back to his desk, sat down, and picked up his pen and the paper he had been writing on when she came into the room, and then said quietly, very quietly:

"All right, Mom. The job's out."

He could feel her standing and looking at him. But he didn't turn to her. He began to write.

Finally she went out of the room.

4

*He didn't sleep well that night. Near morning
he found himself sitting up in bed as if listening
for something. He didn't know what it was that
had awakened him. The house was noiseless.
Then he got up and went to the front window
and lifted the shade and looked out. The street
was silent and dim. The distant trees were
blurred. He went back to his sleep and dreamed
that he and his mother were fighting over a black
overcoat. Then a figure that looked like Mr. Warfield came between them and grabbed the overcoat from their hands and ran off. He held the
coat high as he ran, and the wind caught it and
waved it like a huge, ominous flag.
Black against a smoky sky.
When Danny awoke again, the sunlight was
streaming into his room.*

"Danny."

It was his mother's voice, out in the hallway.
He went to the closed door — he always closed
his door when he slept at night — and opened
it.

"Carol. She's on the phone."

"Oh."

He stood looking at his mother. A touch of sadness lingered about her. It came to him then that she had not slept well, and he was about to say to her, "Did you ever get the overcoat back from Mr. Warfield?" when he realized the absurdity of it all, and said nothing.

"She's on the phone, Danny," his mother said again.

"Okay," he said gently.

He went past her to the phone in the hallway and sat down at the little table that his father had once made. Danny's hand felt the soft polish of the wood as he picked up the receiver. He heard his mother go off to her room and silently close the door.

"Hello?"

"Hello, Danny. I wake you?"

"Uh-huh."

"It's past ten."

"Is it?"

"That's right. Twenty past ten."

"Oh."

"What are your plans?"

"Plans?"

"The sun's out. Strong."

"Oh."

"Are you awake?"

"Yes."

Then he heard her laughter that always seemed to warm him. It was low and full and young.

He listened to it and began to smile.

"Sure you're awake?"

"Sure."

"So what do you want to do?"

"Hadn't given it a thought."

"Okay. Let me give you some."

And he suddenly remembered. It took the smile away from him.

"I've got to go to the museum," he said.

"Museum?"

"Uh-huh."

"On a day like today?"

"Got to."

"Today? With the sun out as it is?"

He looked down the hallway to the living-room window. The sun pushed through it and tumbled over the chairs and rug.

"Who knows when we'll get another day like this, Danny." Her voice was vibrant. "Winter is coming on. Snow, Danny. Snow and dismal days. Rain and sleet."

She was a tall girl, and she wore her hair long, honeyblonde and long. It swept down over her shoulders and danced against her straight back as she walked. When she read in class, she put on large shell glasses, and it made her look serene and sure of herself, her movements slow and confident; it made her darting hazel eyes mature and deepen, it made her look like the grown sedate woman she would become.

But when she walked with him, she was a young, glowing girl.

"Put your hand out and feel the air. Just feel it. Cup your hand and feel it glow. Will make you want to sing."

She wrote poetry for the school literary magazine. It was simple and direct, just as she was.

"We can take the ferry to Staten Island and go to Silver Lake Park," she said.

"We could."

"We could take our rackets along."

"Yeah."

"Well?"

He thought and then shook his head somberly.

"Well?" she asked again.

He started to shake his head again, and then right in the middle of it he realized that she couldn't see him, and he started to laugh. For some reason he started to laugh. She started to laugh with him.

"Well?" she said again, still laughing and not asking him why they were laughing.

"I don't know," he said, still laughing.

"Is it schoolwork?"

"An assignment," he said as the laughter died away.

"You couldn't put it off till Monday?"

He thought of the walls of the classroom and didn't answer. The high dun walls with the shadows long against them and the teacher's voice, harsh and cutting.

"I guess you can't put it off," she said, and there was disappointment in her voice.

"I can't," he said.

He could see the lips press tight, and the fire come to the hazel eyes, the toss of the long, swishing hair.

"How about tonight?" he asked. "Maybe we can get together for tonight?"

"Maybe."

"Well?"

There was a silence. Then she said, "Don't know what my plans are going to be for today. I have to settle today first, Danny."

"Oh."

"Might be with the same fellow at night. Don't know."

"Yeah," he said gloomily.

"I just said no to somebody, and now I've got to call him and say yes."

"Sorry to put you in that position."

"I was sure you'd want to spend the day with me so I said no to him."

"I do want to spend the day with you."

"But you're not."

"I explained to you, Carol."

"You did."

Out on Troop Place he could hear the sounds of some kids playing touch football. The sound of the ball hitting the pavement bounded up to him. His hand reached out instinctively to catch it, then dropped back to his side.

"What museum are you going to?" she asked.

"Brooklyn."

"What for?"

"See the Van Gogh exhibit. The one with the new painting they just found. It's an assignment, and I've got to do it."

"I saw it already. It's a good one. I liked it very much."

"You're a square."

She laughed. He smiled when he heard the warm rise and fall of her voice.

"You should see more art, Danny. The pop stuff around is alive. Sends me."

"I'll stick with science. I'm going to teach it."

"So stick to it and teach it. But what has that to do with liking art?"

"Listen. It's like football. Either you take to it or you don't. I don't take to art."

"You've never given it a chance. So how can you tell what you like and what you don't like?"

"I know."

"I wonder if you really know what's inside you, Danny?" she said.

It was the way she said it, softly and directly, that hit into him. They had been bantering each other, just making talk, and she had said it.

"I wonder if you really know what's inside you, Danny?"

The words echoed within him. He suddenly saw a long, lonely day stretching ahead of him. He wanted to plead with her to come with him. But he just sat there holding the telephone and rubbing his hand over the polished surface of the little table. Thinking of his father and what a lonely man he had been.

"So you're going to the museum?"

"Yes," he said.

There was a pause.

"Today is not our day," she said.

"It isn't."

"So let's forget it. Like I never called."

"Okay."

"Okay," she said with a sigh. "Cool it, man."

"Cool it, man," he said.

He waited for the sound of the click, and then he slowly put down the receiver. Outside, the kids on Troop Place still played touch football.

5

He once heard a song, and he didn't know where, but he was sure he had heard it, heard it sung in a low whining voice against the slow thrumming of the low strings of an old guitar, and the words ran like this:

Deathman, do not follow me
Deathman, do not follow me
You may be good
You may be evil
But do not follow me.
Deathman.
You may be clouds
You may be sun
But do not follow me.
Deathman.
You may be blood
You may be water
But do not follow me.
Deathman.
You may be blood.
Deathman.

Now, as he stood in front of the looming stone building of the Brooklyn Museum, the words and the melody came back to him. For the life of

*him he couldn't make out why they should come
to him now.*
*Later, much later, days later, and nights later, he
understood.*

The song stayed with him, like a silver thread,
while he climbed the five smooth granite stair-
cases — the elevators were too crowded — then
walked through the huge circular Sculpture Court
and into the Early American art galleries,
through the Renaissance art gallery, and then
through an arch and into the European art room.
Then he saw the painting and the people hud-
dled about it, and as he got closer the song faded
and vanished.

And with the vanishing he felt a strange release and a lightening, as if the song had leaden
weight and now the weight had been taken off
his chest and he could breathe freely again. For
a moment he stood there enjoying the sense of
release and wondering about it; then he looked
at the painting. He saw only a meaningless swirl
of bright colors.

It disappointed him.

He wondered why the people were there,
crowded into the gallery, when outside the sun
was shining and the day was filled with a simple
beauty. He shrugged his shoulders, moved a bit
away from the painting, and began to read the
text of a large card that had been placed on an
easel. The card contained background material
about Vincent Van Gogh and the painting.

He began to write in a small notebook he had
brought along with him. Danny underlined that

the painting had been recently found in an attic of a farmhouse. The farmhouse was in the vicinity of Arles, a community in the south of France. He also noted that Vincent Van Gogh had lived for a time in Arles and had done some of his best painting there.

He paused for awhile when he read that Van Gogh had once lived in the Borinage, with Belgian miners. This man had tried to help the miners in their struggle against poverty and had been defeated. Strange flickering thoughts sped through him. One of them was of his father's once telling him that he wanted to be a lawyer in order to help people — people like the miners of West Virginia, who were suffering and deprived. For an instant he felt close to Vincent Van Gogh.

Then he began to write again. As he wrote, he found himself listening to the voice of a man who stood beside him — listening and beginning to copy down each word the man said. Even the unimportant, casual words.

The man was talking to a woman.

". . . one of the finest Van Gogh's I've ever seen. To think that this painting lay in an attic all these years."

"It's beautiful," the woman said.

"Beautiful?" he shook his head. "Impressive. Not beautiful. Impressive. Once seen, it's never forgotten."

"It has beauty."

"Power."

Danny turned and looked up at the man. He was tall, taller than Danny and much leaner.

He had a narrow, angular face, with a long nose and thin lips. His hair was white and silky, combed neatly away from a high, severe forehead. His eyes were brown, deep brown; quiet, appraising eyes.

He wore a dark suit that had a slight sheen to it. It fit his lean body gracefully. In his delicate hand he carried a long, knobby cane. The cane was out of keeping with the long, patrician figure and the silky white hair and the thin, fine lips. It was rough and heavy — almost peasant-like in its solidity.

The woman was younger than the man and expensively dressed.

"Not beauty," the man murmured, and said it slowly and low, as if talking to himself. "Not beauty. Anguish perhaps. A cry of color against the drab viciousness of our world. A — "

He stopped as he saw Danny standing and listening to him intently, his pencil poised. For an instant the brown eyes of the man shaded, his patrician face seemed to grow severe, and then he suddenly laughed, a low, pleasant laugh.

"Have you been copying what I've said?"

Danny didn't answer. He just stood there looking at the man.

"What did you write?" the woman asked.

She had gray hair, but her face was pert and young. She appeared to be twenty years younger than the man, possibly in her forties.

"Nothing much," Danny said, feeling uncomfortable.

"That it has power or beauty?"

"Power," Danny said.

The man's thin nostril's quivered with satisfaction as he turned to the woman.

"There," he said.

He turned back to Danny.

"Come a bit closer to the painting, and I'll tell you more about it. That's if you want me to. Evidently you have a school assignment. Am I right?"

"Yes."

"Well, perhaps I can help you get a good mark."

He drew Danny almost in front of the painting. The woman with the sleek gray hair moved near him and listened with a casual, almost indifferent amusement, as if she had heard what he was to say time and time again before.

"First, let me tell you how far I've come to see this very painting." He paused and looked about him, noting that some of the people standing around were listening. This seemed to please him. Then he said quietly:

"Mrs. Collingwood and I flew in from Seattle. Just to see this Van Gogh. We're flying back Monday."

"You came just to see this?"

"Just this. I'm sure there are people who have come from greater distances. This painting is a jewel."

Danny was silent.

"A jewel. The Brooklyn Museum helped to find this jewel. Now they have the honor of being the first to show it in America. Don't you feel proud of your museum?"

Danny nodded.

The man looked at him, a quiet, almost ironic smile playing on his thin, fine lips.

"Are you an art critic?" Danny asked.

"No. Merely a man who loves art. As you see so many others do."

He said that with a quiet, expressive gesture at the crowded gallery.

"What's there about this painting that appeals to you so much?" Danny asked.

"Appeals to me? Well, I could give you a lecture on art. But I won't."

His delicate hand went to his white hair and stroked it as he spoke. Slow, smoothing strokes.

Later, much later, Danny would remember that hand. And the slow, smoothing strokes.

"Better that I point out to you that you haven't even looked at this painting. I believe you should."

"I did look at it," Danny said.

"I question that," the man said, his eyes probing and studying Danny. "You glanced and ran."

Danny flushed. He never thought the man was aware of that.

The man let his hand fall to his side and laughed, a quiet melodic laugh.

"It's so, isn't it?"

Danny didn't speak.

"It is so. The very first thing you did was to snatch out your copybook and start writing down notes. Furiously. As if you were in some lecture hall and the professor had begun to speak."

He paused and looked about him at the people who had come closer to them. A cluster. He had taken on the role of art lecturer, and they had accepted it easily.

"Taking notes. But that should be the last thing you should do when you come to a gallery to see paintings. You should come to experience them. To enjoy them. The same as you would enjoy a good movie, a good television program, a good book."

He paused and studied Danny again, this time going over his figure appraisingly.

"Or a good football game," he softly added. "Do you like football?"

"I play it."

"I thought so. For your school team?"

"Yes."

"I'll bet you're a fine player."

Danny was silent.

"What position do you play?"

"Quarterback."

The man nodded approvingly.

"You're a leader. I like men who lead. What is your name?"

"Danny."

"Danny what?"

"Danny Morgan."

"A fine Welsh name. Are you Welsh?"

"On my father's side," Danny said, and as he did, he realized that this was the first time he had told that to anybody in a long time.

"Glad to meet you, Danny."

The man slightly bent his body forward to Danny and held out his hand. The fingers, the long tapering fingers were curved in. Danny thought immediately of the Greek patricians he used to read about when he was younger and liked to read all about Athens.

"I'm Walter Collingwood, and this is my wife Marian."

Danny shook the man's hand and smiled at Mrs. Collingwood.

"I'm pleased to meet you, Danny," she said in a warm voice.

She turned her face fully to him as she spoke, and a cold chill suddenly dashed through him. A long, twisting scar ran down the side of her face that had been away from him, from ear to chin.

He stared at the scar — stared and wondered what terrible accident had so disfigured her. He could almost hear her scream of pain as the scar was torn into the young living flesh — hear the scream and see the blood spurt out.

Then he heard a voice, low and commanding.

"Let's look at the painting, Danny."

Danny flushed guiltily and turned from the woman and back to the man. Collingwood's eyes were severe and cold. The lips pressed together.

"The painting," the man said again.

Then the coldness left his eyes, the lips began to smile gently again, the hand that had gripped the cane tightly, ever so tightly that the knuckles showed white, now relaxed and wavered about the knob.

"Look at the painting, lad."

His voice was now gentle and eager, as if he wanted to give something to Danny, something that was priceless, something that he would carry with him for the rest of his long life to come.

The man touched Danny slightly on the shoulder. Danny turned with the touch and looked fully at the painting. And for the first time he really saw it. Something in the sudden sight of the scar, something in the voice of the man, in the touch on the shoulder, had opened up a new area of feeling within him — of feeling and of sight.

There before him stretched a night scene. A swirly, stormy night, yet bright and glowing with stars that moved like fireballs across a sky. Beneath the heaving sky was the fierce quietness of a huge field of wheat stretching far and far to the end of time, waving and yet so still, each stalk of wheat so bright and so still, still.

A stormy night. And yet within the very eye of the storm Danny felt — and could not find why he felt it, for it was not there in the painting of the colors, nor in the swirling brushstrokes of deep blues and violent yellows — he felt in the center of all the raging violence a deep serenity of spirit, of peace, a peace he had never before known in all his life.

It was a new feeling for him.

"You see the painting," the man said with delight. "You see it. It's there in your eyes, in the way you're standing."

Danny didn't say anything. His eyes swept over the canvas, experiencing every little square of it. And yet he didn't know why. He didn't know why.

"It's like trying to explain the beauty of a blackbird flying high into the sun over the summer lake. You see every little sparkle on the wing and you feel the flight of the bird. But you can't tell it to anyone. There are no words.

"He sees it, Marian," the man whispered to the woman.

She nodded.

Danny still looked at the painting and still didn't speak. Collingwood stood close by him, silent.

"It doesn't have a title," he finally said.

"What would you call it, Danny?"

"Heartbreak," Danny said instantly.

"Heartbreak?"

"Why that?" Mrs. Collingwood asked.

Danny shrugged. For the moment he didn't know why. The word had sprung from some inner depth.

"Heartbreak," Collingwood murmured.

He was now fully concentrated upon the painting. He stood there, leaning forward a bit, his weight on the long, knobby cane. Suddenly he slowly nodded, his brown eyes gentle. Nodded but still stood there, concentrated.

"Yes," he said. "I can understand your title."

He paused and nodded his white head slowly.

"It's the cry of the spirit against the cruelty of harsh, savage nature."

"I didn't mean that," Danny said.

"No?"

"It wasn't that. It's something else."

Collingwood had turned to Danny.

"What?"

"I can't explain."

"Perhaps Van Gogh can."

56

Danny looked back to the painting, studying it again and again, the way the sky moved over stalks of wheat that stood so silently, so still, even thought they were waving in a fierce wind.

Suddenly he felt that he could explain the title. The words hovered on the tip of his tongue, hovered and were lost again. And he realized that it was useless to try. Just as useless as to try to explain the flight of the bird.

"Heartbreak," Collingwood said reflectively.

"Storm," a man in the group about them said.

"Night scene," another submitted.

A discussion broke out, and the Collingwoods joined in. Danny stood silently, not listening to a word, just looking every now and then at the painting — looking and wondering why it had reached into him and gripped his very soul.

Long after he had left the museum and the company of the Collingwoods, he still thought of that.

6

He woke up that night, and he went to the front
window, his feet padding softly over the cold
floor.

He looked out at the night sky and thought of
the painting. Below him, Troop Place was silent
and cold. The three-story houses with their front
gardens — three-story houses that once were
private and now were let out as apartments —
looked like giant stone figures with windowed
eyes, the corner lights glancing off them. The
gardens were bare of leaves and grass and
flowers, waiting for the first strike of winter.

He thought of the painting and of Walter Collingwood. He had walked with the Collingwoods
down the granite stairway, staircase after staircase, the cane tapping harshly every now and
then against the smooth stone, till they got to the
bottom. Collingwood had turned to him, asked
him where he lived, and smiled when Danny told
him. Then Mrs. Collingwood had patted him
gently, her eyes warm upon him, her face slightly averted so that he could not see her scar.

Then they both had turned and walked out of the
museum.

Now as he stood looking at the night sky, the stars splashed across it, he remembered standing in the museum, by the shadowy checkroom, standing and watching the two figures as they walked out through the bronze doorway and into the sudden sunlight.

They were out of his life, he thought then.

But Collingwood stopped short and glanced back; as if he seemed to know what Danny was thinking. The woman had not stopped with him, but kept walking straight ahead into the sunny day. Collingwood lifted his hand in farewell and then walked after the woman. The last Danny saw of him was the cold glint of light on the knobby cane.

Like the glint of fierce starlight that now struck the glass of the front window of his room — struck through and onto the floor, lighting it into white flame. He stood there enveloped in the strange brightness, thinking of the painting, of the Collingwoods, of Mr. Warfield.

Finally, he pulled the shade down and blotted out the night.

He slept fitfully.

In the morning he called Carol.

"I wake you?"

"No."

But she sounded sleepy.

"You go out last night?"

"Uh-huh."

"Have a good time?"

"So-so."

He liked that, but it didn't show in his voice.

"What did you do?"

"Nothing much."

He sat there at the little telephone table and wondered why he liked to sit and talk to her.

"You go to the museum, Danny?"

"Uh-huh."

"Well?"

"Well what?"

"Did you like the painting?"

"Which one?"

"Cool it, man," she said.

He smiled.

"Yes, I liked it," he said.

"I told you that you would."

"That's right. You did."

"You're just stubborn. Like all men."

He let the word "men" sink in for awhile. He liked that.

"Plain stubborn," he heard her say again.

His mother went by him on the way to the kitchen. He smiled up at her.

"Morning, Danny," she whispered.

She seemed glad that he was smiling.

"Morning," he whispered back.

He watched her tall figure till it disappeared.

"You there, Danny?" he heard Carol ask.

He spoke quickly into the phone.

"I'm there."

But he thought of his mother and of the argument they'd had over the job in the drugstore. It brought back a bit of the bitterness and at the same time it made him feel even more tender to both Carol and his mother. A crazy-mixed-up feeling, he thought to himself, and the words of a song popped into his mind as he spoke to Carol.

"I'm waiting for you to say something, Carol."

"For me?"

"Uh-huh."

The melody bounced along in his mind. He tapped his fingers on the table in a gay rhythm.

"What did you call me for?"

He stopped tapping. But the bubbling lightness remained within. It was a crazy-mixed-up feeling.

"Call you?" he asked.

"That's right. You woke me up."

"But you said I didn't wake you."

"Did I?"

"Right at the beginning of our conversation."

"I don't remember saying that."

"But I do."

He tapped it out on the table in rhythmic emphasis.

"I definitely do."

"You're not calling me a liar, Danny?"

Confronted with this, he tapped and considered it.

"Well, are you?" she asked.

"Of course not, Carol," he said.

There was a pause. The melody still bounced along.

"So you liked the painting," she said.

"Uh-huh."

"I wish you wouldn't uh-huh me so much, Danny."

"I uh-huh you? You've been uh-huhing me all way through, Carol."

"I never said one uh-huh. Not one."

"I heard no less than three."

"Well, tell me, Mr. Man. Just tell me."

He paused.

"I can't remember," he said.

He heard her laugh.

"What are you laughing about?" he asked.

"Our conversation. Just doesn't make sense."

He began to laugh, too.

"It doesn't."

"It's wild, man," she said.

"It's wild, man," he said.

"You want to see me today?"

"Yes."

"Okay. I think I can swing it."

"Good."

"Where do you want to go?"

"Anywhere you say."

"How's the weather?"

"Don't know. How is it?"

"Don't know. I asked you first."

"Maybe I ought to look out the window and see."

"Maybe you should."

"Hold on."

"Okay."

He got up from the table and went down the hallway to the side window, the narrow side window. He pulled up the shade, and the bubbling lightness that was in him vanished as he looked out.

The day was cold.

A beginning-of-winter day, as if yesterday's

brilliance had never existed and never would again.

He stood there gazing grimly at the smoky clouds heavy on the sky, loading it down close to earth. And then he gazed at the bare outlines of the distant trees in the shadowy park.

He went back to the phone.

"Looks rotten out."

"Oh," she said, and her voice fell.

"Thought we'd get out in the sun. But there is none."

"That's what I tried to tell you yesterday."

"I know."

"You should've listened to me, Danny. We could've gone to Silver Lake and had a ball."

He was silent.

He heard her sigh, and he knew that she didn't have a good time yesterday. He thought of Mr. Warfield with a sudden hot anger.

"Well, what say?"

"It's up to you, Carol."

"Why put it up to me?"

"Because I'll do anything you want. That's why."

"Anything?"

"Anything."

"How about a walk on the boardwalk?"

"Atlantic City?"

"Coney Island."

"That's what I said."

"That's what I heard."

He laughed. He was getting bouncy again.

"I'll wear my straw hat and bring along a cane," he said.

"Do. Please do."

"It's a date?"

"Check."

"I'll pick you up what time?"

"Make it twoish."

"Why not oneish? We'll have more time together."

"Because my father needs me."

"To help at an operation?"

Her father was a surgeon, a short, brisk, kindly man who was fond of Danny and often tried to interest him in a medical career.

"No. To help tie his bow tie. He's going to a wedding."

"What's the matter with Mother?"

"Mother will have nail polish on."

"Do help Father with his tie."

"I will do."

He tapped on the table lightheartedly. His mother came by and smiled at him. Danny winked at her.

"Okay. I'll be there at two," he said into the phone.

"I'll be waiting."

"Good."

There was a pause. He could see her sitting on the soft blue sofa, her legs curled up under her.

"Are we out of words, Danny?"

"Looks like it."

"Okay. Hit the receiver, man."

He sat there for a long time, just thinking of her.

7

Just as he was leaving the house, he met the messenger coming up the steep flight of steps. He was an old, wizened little man, with a face like a walnut, all shriveled in. He wore an old battered Western Union cap, and he had a package. It was for Daniel Morgan, 33 Troop Place. He gave it to Danny, closed the dime tip in his tight, bony hand, and then went down the stairs and out of Danny's life.

Later, much later, Danny saw that it was impossible for any messenger to get out of one's life. Like in a Greek play of blood and violence, the little old man with the face all lined and yellow like a walnut was a messenger sent by the gods. Blown in by fate.

Grim fate.

The only thing was that Danny didn't know it then. The same way that none of us knows when the Deathman is around.

Until he wants us to know. Then we know.

"A book?" Carol asked.

"That's right," he said.

They were sitting on the boardwalk looking out

at the green sea. It was an angry sea that stretched out to a pencil-thin horizon. Every now and then the whitecaps rode along it, shaking their heads like mad horses — mad white horses that finally exploded in a shower of foam.

"A book about what?"

"About Van Gogh."

"His life?"

"Uh-huh."

There was a card in the package: "Do hope you will enjoy reading this book. We are leaving this evening for Seattle. Please don't forget us. Walter and Marian Collingwood."

Danny looked out across the sea, and he thought of the lean man with the knobby cane and of the woman with the scar that ran from her ear to her chin. A white horse exploded just a few feet from the beach with a mighty roar.

"They seem to be nice people," Carol said.

A breeze had come up and was running through her long hair, wisping it over her clear forehead.

"Real nice people, Danny."

He turned from the sea and looked at her.

"Yes. They seem to be."

She glanced questioningly at him.

"Why do you say seem?"

He shrugged.

"I think it was a fine thing to do. Send a book to a fellow they met just once."

He sat silently.

"Well, wasn't it?"

"I guess it was."

"Why do you say guess?"

He shrugged again. He really didn't know what was nagging him inside, what kept him from opening up and agreeing that the Collingwoods were fine people. She was right. They had met him only once, had seen him but a short time, and now they had gone to the trouble and expense of sending him a gift.

"Why, Danny?"

She put her hand to her hair and smoothed it down slowly, and he instantly remembered Collingwood's lean hand smoothing down the silky white hair, slowly remembered and was silent.

"There's something locked away in you, Danny," she said.

He turned from her searching gaze, turned and found a sail among the angry waves. It was far, far out. Just where the horizon thinned into a precise line against a heavy, gray sky.

"Always locked away," he heard her say.

Her words were like leaves falling off a tree. There was a sadness to them, and he felt it.

"Part of you is always locked away. Nobody ever touches it. Nobody."

Leaves. Falling leaves.

"Nobody," he murmured, so low that she couldn't hear it.

"Long as I know you, Danny, that's how it's been. I've always felt it. From the very beginning. And I can't understand it. I just can't."

"I guess I'm not like other fellows," he said, still following the sail riding the green waves, way, way out, riding, glimmering, and almost blurring out from view at times, then glimmering right back in again.

"I guess I'm not like other fellows," he repeated.

A couple passed by them, and then their footsteps thudding along the wood of the boardwalk faded out. Danny and Carol were alone again. The benches before and ahead of them were empty. Strung in an empty line against a railing that was iron and bare.

"Why aren't you like other fellows?" she asked.

They had wandered almost to the end of the Island, where few went in cold weather, where the beach jutted out into the sea and the boardwalk curved with it.

"I don't know why," he finally said. "Maybe losing a father does it to you. I don't know why."

He clenched and unclenched his hand.

"But even that isn't the answer," he said. "Even that. Other fellows have lost fathers and have gone on. No real change in them. I don't know. I really don't know." He rested his long legs on the railing. Sat back and rested his legs and looked away from the glimmering sail and up into the heavy sky. His hair fluttered in the sharp breeze, almost like a flag.

"Mr. Warfield calls me a loner."

"When? When did he say that?"

"The other day."

"He talks too much."

"I guess he does."

He turned from the sky and down to her.

68

She's pretty, he thought to himself. She's very pretty. Especially when she's angry.

"That's a cruel thing to say to anyone."

"Cruel?"

"Yes, Danny."

He shrugged.

"He's a good teacher, but he can be a louse sometimes," she said.

"All teachers can be louses at times," Danny said.

"Well, it's a damn shame when he is. Because he's a good teacher and a decent person."

"I wonder how I'm going to be when I get to teach," Danny said.

"Want me to tell you?"

He shook his head and laughed.

"Why not? Chicken?"

"Sure am."

They both laughed together. He put his hand over hers. She let it rest there. They sat close and looked out to the sea. For a long time they sat there, just feeling good being close to each other, and seeing water and sky, and feeling the wind rise against them.

"Sometimes I don't sleep well," he said. "Sometimes I get afraid."

She was silent, thinking over what he had revealed about himself.

"I guess it's part of being a loner. In the daytime you make it all right. You get away with it. But sometimes at night, I wake up. The past few nights I've been waking up. . . ." His voice trailed off into the rising wind.

He felt her kiss against his cheek. A soft, tentative kiss. It told him of her trying to understand what was within him.

"We all have fears, Danny," she said.

He nodded.

"It's a nervous world."

He nodded again and waited for her to speak more.

"You turn on a television show, and then it's interrupted, and there you have a news bulletin announcing a new crisis. A nervous world."

"I sometimes wonder if we're going to make it."

He felt her warm hand in his.

"I sometimes wonder if we're not going to blow up like those waves. Just blow up and disappear like we were never here."

They were silent.

"We were here, Danny," she said softly.

Her words seemed to go through him and then out and over the entire ocean. Echoing again and again.

We were here.

We were here.

We were here.

"My father used to feel the same way, Carol."

"Did he?"

"Uh-huh."

The wind started blowing into the sand. Blowing it up and whirling it over the beach and over the ocean.

"With all the disappointments he had, still he felt the same way. That we would make it in the long run."

"He must've been a fine man, Danny."

Danny watched the sand a while. Then he said quietly:

"He was."

He watched the wind and the sand a little longer, watched how the wind fiercely dug into the sand and threw it at will wherever it wished, and then suddenly he said in a low, despairing voice:

"But what good did it do him, Carol?"

"Danny," she said softly.

He got up and shook his head bitterly.

"He got sick and died."

She rose and stood by him.

"Died. And all his plans and hopes went down with him. So what good was it, Carol? What good?"

She let him talk it out.

"Fate just takes you by the neck and does what it wants. I get scared. Real scared. I have plans, too."

"They'll work out, Danny."

"How do you know?"

"I know."

"Are you God?"

She was silent.

"Even He doesn't know anymore, Carol. Even He."

He waved his hand bitterly at the ocean. Waved it and then let it fall helplessly to his side.

Then he said softly:

"Lately I feel more scared than I've ever been. I don't know why. I don't know what it is."

"You don't?"

"No."

Then he added in a low, low voice, "I just feel that something is closing in on me."

She looked sharply and searchingly at him.

"No," he said, smiling bitterly. "I'm not going off my rocker, Carol. It's not that."

"I didn't think it was, Danny."

"It was in your eyes."

The wind began to blow about them.

"Let's walk," he said.

"All right."

After awhile he turned to her with a sad smile.

"I guess you're sorry you came along today."

"No, Danny. No."

She drew his arm about her. They kissed. Then they walked to the very end of the boardwalk, where the wind was at its fiercest.

There they kissed again.

8

Just as he was about to fall asleep he heard the
low sound of a car coming to a stop just across the
street. He lay there waiting for the sound of the
metal door opening and of voices, but he heard
nothing

Nothing.

Finally, he got out of bed and went to the window, lifted the shade a bit and peered out into
the starless night. The car was a long black limousine, and it seemed to him that there were
three figures seated in it. Two in the back and
one in the front.

The one in the front had on a chauffeur's uni-
form. He could see that because of the glancing
light of the street lamp as it fell across the front
of the car, but the rest of the car was in darkness.
Utter darkness.

Then he thought he could see the head of the
person sitting in the back, the person closest to
him.

It sent a strange, almost weird feeling racing
through him. After awhile the car started up and
almost silently drove off. As it did, it passed un-

*der the street lamp for an instant, and he could
see — he could swear that he could see — the
glint of a knobby cane.*

"You can sit down, Morgan."

Danny slowly sat down, his face white. Mr.
Warfield's eyes bored into him. The teacher's jaw
muscles worked, and his nostrils were wide.

Then he turned to the rest of the class and said
curtly:

"Class dismissed."

As the class silently filed out, he motioned
grimly to Danny to remain seated. Then when
the room was empty of all but the two, he went
to the doors and closed them.

First one and then the other.

"All right, Morgan, let's have this out once and
for all."

Mr. Warfield eased his rugged body into a seat
close to Danny and thrust his head forward like
a bull.

"Just what are you trying to pull on me?" he
asked almost savagely.

Danny felt his body tighten as it did at the
start of a football game, but his voice came out
quiet and even.

"I told you, Mr. Warfield, that I did go to that
museum. I also told you that I had left my notes
at home. I'm not trying to pull anything on you."

"You did your best to make a fool out of me
before the rest of the class."

"That's not so."

"You dare say that to me?"

"Yes."

74

"You can be brazen, too, can't you?"

"I did not try to make a fool out of you."

"That's what you say."

"That's what I say, Mr. Warfield."

The teacher suddenly got up and walked away. He went to one of the large windows and looked out, his broad back to Danny, straight and hard like a wall. Danny stared at it and felt a hot anger rise in him — anger at Mr. Warfield and at himself. But mostly at himself.

How the devil could he have left those notes home? After all the work he did on them. To have the report all made out and then to forget it on his desk in his bedroom. To get up late and rush out of the house without breakfast and without the report. It was because of that damned black car that he woke up late. It had kept him up most of the night thinking about it.

The car.

Then to stand up in class and make a mess of the whole business. He couldn't talk about the painting and make sense. He got all mixed up. What had happened to him? The more Mr. Warfield jumped on him, the more mixed up he got. But he knew the painting, had thought about it again and again. Knew every inch of its canvas, its heart, its spirit. Knew it better than anyone who had ever seen it before.

Yes, better than anyone.

"I know that painting better than anybody who's ever seen it."

The teacher turned about.

"That's right," Danny said fiercely.

"I don't believe you were even there."

"Then damn you, don't believe it!" Danny shouted.

The two stared at each other in silence. Danny had risen when he spoke, now he slowly sat down, slowly, very slowly. A tired look came over Mr. Warfield's face. When he spoke, his voice was muted.

"If you want to curse," he said, "curse and get it out of your system. I won't take any action against you."

"I don't want to curse," Danny said.

"Call me names. Tell me what you think of me. It's open house."

Danny was silent.

"Say what you want to say."

"I've said it."

The teacher looked away from the pupil and then muttered wearily:

"They don't pay enough for this job. There's just not enough money."

"You still don't believe me," Danny said.

"No," Mr. Warfield said grimly. "You can put on whatever act you want, I don't believe you."

"It's no act."

"Whatever little you know about that painting you've picked up from your classmates."

"What?"

"I saw you talking to George Cheever before class."

"So?"

"Did he tell you about the painting?"

Danny hesitated.

"Well, did he?"

"We spoke about it. A few words and then the bell rang."

"I see."

"No, you don't see. That's the whole trouble. You don't want to see."

"Because you've been lying to me."

"No. I've been telling the truth."

"Then I'm the liar?"

"If you say I didn't go to that museum, then you are."

Mr. Warfield's head shot up. His eyes blazed at Danny.

"You're getting under my skin, Morgan."

"That's not my fault," Danny said.

"What?"

"Not mine."

"I've been up against teacher-baiters before. Guys who just hate teachers because they're teachers. Some of them were big, tough athletes. Muscle men but no heart, no brains, no sense of human dignity. Teacher-baiters. I never thought you would turn out to be one. Never."

"If I am one, then it's you who's made me."

"I'm warning you, Morgan. I'll take you out on that football field and beat some sense into you myself if that's what you want."

His voice rose. "I'll take you out now."

He moved a few steps toward Danny, his whole body thrust forward. Then he seemed to catch hold of himself, and he breathed out heavily and turned abruptly away. He slowly sat down again and looked at his two hands — held them up and stared at them, as if he were alone in the room, with the winter sun coming through the window and falling on the two thick-fingered hands lighting the knuckles and leaving the rest in flecked shadow.

"I killed with these hands," he said. "I'm a man who loves beauty and art and music, and yet I killed with these hands. More than once."

He slowly put his hands down.

There was a great silence. Danny felt it pervade the whole building, as if all voices had stopped and were listening to Mr. Warfield.

"More than once," he whispered.

His voice died away, and the silence rushed in again. The teacher sat there staring into space as if seeing again the scenes of violence and blood that he had lived through. Suddenly he became aware that Danny was in the room with him. He turned and looked at the youth. His shadow lay heavy on the wall — heavy yet sharply outlined.

Then Danny heard him say: "Killed so that you and other kids like you could have your chance at art and beauty and music. So that some damned barbarians shouldn't take your life and snuff out all that was decent and worthwhile in it. Destroy all the joy and goodness that is coming to you."

His voice became hard and jagged as steel.

"Morgan, you'll get the hell to that museum and see that painting and come in with that report. Do you hear me?"

He rose. Then took out his pen and small white pad. He spoke to Danny as he wrote on the white pad.

"You'll have the guard sign this. The one who stands directly by the painting. When I see his signature, I'll know you were there."

He ripped the note from the pad and handed it to Danny.

"Don't try to fool me again, Morgan. I know the guard, so don't think you can have one of your friends sign this for you."

Danny silently put the note into his pocket.

"You still have time. So get off your butt and get going."

His scarred hand hit the desk with explosive force.

"Now."

When Danny left the room he glanced back. The teacher was standing in the center of the room, looking down at his two hands.

Outside the day was beginning to die.

9

It was dark and cold when Danny finished the long walk from the school to the museum. He hurried through the high bronze doorway and into the warmth of the huge stone building. He paused by the sign which said that the museum would be open till nine o'clock during the special Van Gogh exhibit, checked his coat, and then walked to the elevator.

It was while he stood in the small elevator car, pressed back by the crowd, that he thought of George and Carol. It would've been good to have one of them along with him. Just someone to talk to, to help ease the feeling of anger and resentment that now swept through him.

But as he left the elevator at the fifth floor and started to walk through the galleries, he found something strange happening to him. He found that as he came closer and closer to where the Van Gogh painting was, his blood began to thrill, his heart to beat faster. He stopped for a moment to question what was happening to him — to try to understand it.

Why? Why did he feel this way? What was

there in the painting that so surely reached into him and spoke to his very soul? Spoke with so much beauty and heartbreak?

Heartbreak. That's what he had called the work.

The room was crowded, almost as much as it had been on Saturday afternoon, and he caught himself looking about for the Collingwoods and expecting to hear their voices.

But they were not there.

He saw the guard standing near the painting. He was a little, bald-headed man with twinkling blue eyes. He was chuckling and pointing out something interesting on the canvas. The people standing near him nodded in agreement.

Danny caught the words "Does it with a few brushstrokes. A world in a few . . ." Then the rest of the words were lost in the general noise of the room. He walked closer to the painting and then stood directly in front of it.

The very instant that he did, he knew that something was wrong.

He stood there, his blood turning cold.

For deep within him was the knowledge that the painting he now saw was not the one he had called Heartbreak.

Though in every detail it was the same, yet it was not the same.

This painting was a fake, a lie.

But what was more appalling than that, no one seemed to know it.

PART TWO

DEATHMAN, DO NOT FOLLOW ME

10

Once when he was a small boy he sat at the circus with his father and watched the Antonellis perform high on the high wire, high above the smoky crowd, high till their glistening heads almost touched the dim, gray ceiling of Madison Square Garden.

They began to balance one upon the other and then to walk across the wire — the wire that was stretched like a thread of life across the empty, dark well of the Garden. It was then that he turned to his father and said with a sharp cry,

"They fell!"

His father looked impatiently at him and then turned to stare up at the Antonellis walking across the high wire, balanced one upon the other like a pyramid, while all the people held their breath, but Danny turned again and tugged at his father's jacket sleeve,

"They fell!"

His father wouldn't turn to him anymore.

But Danny had seen the pyramid slowly topple and dissolve, as if in slow motion, topple and dissolve, and then the Antonellis came down, plummeting down, with a whoosh of air, one after the other, and they hit the floor of the arena with a thud and a squirm, and then they became quiet, and dead.

But no one else had seen it.

Only he.

Everybody was still looking up, even his father. And he saw it was no use telling his father again to look down from his balcony seat to see what was happening on the floor below them.

No use to tell him the Antonellis were already fallen and dead.

But all this had happened in Danny's fevered imagination. For days before going to the circus he had talked of nothing else but seeing the Death-Defying Antonellis, Magicians of the High Wire. For days and nights on end he had thought and dreamed about them.

Felt fearful for them.

Once while sitting at breakfast he described their falling with vivid phrases and sound effects. The Great Antonellis falling from their high wire, *falling till they hit the floor. His father had waved his hand that held the circus tickets and laughed. But his mother listened intently till he was done, listened with her eyes shaded by her long tapering hand, and then said quietly that Danny had a very remarkable imagination.*

So it was imagination. All had happened in his imagination. It was illusion, not reality. It couldn't be reality, for everybody still looked up to the glistening white figures, chalk white in the crossing spotlights, high, high up; everybody still watched, with held breath.

Until, suddenly,

the Antonellis did fall.

And the people and his father screamed in terror and heartache, as they hit the floor with a thud.

First one and then another and then another, while all the while the people were standing and screaming, one massive, twisted scream, as if it came from a fatally stricken being.

Illusion had become reality.

Danny found himself screaming with all the others, standing by his father, holding his jacket sleeve and screaming with him.

No one seemed to know it. No one seemed to be aware of what had happened. No one.

Danny stood gazing at the painting, waiting for reality to break with a fury over the entire room. Waiting for people to suddenly begin to gasp and murmur and then shout with a mighty shout:

It's a fake.

This is not Van Gogh.

This is a fraud.

A lie.

Who dared do this crime?

Why was it done?

Why?

But nobody gasped, and nobody shouted, and nobody even turned to Danny. All was as before. The people were standing and chatting and looking. The guard with the bald head and twinkling blue eyes was talking, quietly and sincerely, about the fine points of this outstanding Van Gogh. To his mind, and he had seen a vast number of Van Goghs, here and in Europe — he went to Europe to the galleries on his vacations, he had even spoken to Van Gogh's nephew who was still alive — to his mind, this was at the top, the very top, perhaps the best work that Vincent Van Gogh had ever done.

Danny moved closer to the little group about the small guard. He stood there, no longer listening to the discussion that had broken out, just stood there and tried to get his bearings, to think things through. He wanted the sound and presence of people about him while he thought. For a strange and weird feeling had started within him. A feeling that became a series of sharp and seething questions: Perhaps he was wrong, and everybody else was right. Isn't that more natural? More logical? How could it be possible that they couldn't see what he saw? Maybe he was turning truth upside down. Maybe the question should be, How could it be possible that he, in full possession of his senses, couldn't see what they saw?

That was more like it. Perhaps it was all an illusion, an illusion that this time would not blur into reality. The Antonellis were still up on the high wire, never to fall. Never.

What then? Where did it leave him then? He caught a few words of the discussion, words of reality, words that referred to other paintings that Van Gogh had done — "Starry Night," "The Potato Eaters," "Room at Arles," — words that showed the speakers knew their art and their Van Gogh. Danny listened and then plunged back into the whirling world of his inner thoughts and feelings.

How could he be sure that this was not the true Van Gogh? The one he had seen on Saturday afternoon with the Collingwoods?

The Collingwoods. They would know. They would tell him. If only they were here. If only Mr. Collingwood were standing next to him, leaning on his cane and . . . For some reason Danny felt a chill go through him as he thought of the man with the knobby cane and silky white hair. Then the chill left, and the thoughts and feelings whirled in again.

But even if Collingwood were here, what if he said it was the true Van Gogh? The same one. The very same one. What then? Danny ran his hand through his hair and found it moist, moist with perspiration, yet the room itself was cool and comfortable. He looked at his hand gleaming with wet beads and thought again.

What then? What, after all, did he know about the world of art? He was like a kid lost in a dark forest when it came to paintings. And then again, maybe he knew more than he thought, more than he ever imagined he knew. Mr. Warfield was a good teacher, and things seeped in when one wasn't aware of it.

"Nonsense," he said aloud.

The guard looked questioningly over at Danny, as if puzzled by what Danny had just blurted out. Then he moved his head back to the discussion group. Danny continued to think.

Mr. Warfield. The strong, stocky figure of the teacher loomed up in Danny's consciousness, his eyes large and clear — almost kindly. What if he should ask him to come and see the painting again? He would know. The teacher would know.

But Danny shook his head grimly and cut off the thought. He remembered how Mr. Warfield had treated him before the class, and his resentment now flared up. Danny turned away from the black figure of the teacher and back to his inner questioning. Maybe he did know more than he thought. Maybe he did know his art better than anybody else. In a different way. A different . . .

What a wild thought. And yet why wild? Maybe he knew it in a natural way. Maybe he was a natural. Like in football. They come along once in a generation. Naturals. There's nothing you can teach them. Nothing. They were born with the right reflexes and reactions. They smell a hole in the line before it even opens.

Naturals — they instinctively reach into the truth of things. Know it without knowing why. But they know it. The first man to invent the wheel was a natural. He reached into the heart of science, the very heart of it, and drew out with a sure hand all that was needed, all that was needed for thousands of years to come, on which to build superstructures. All from the wheel. All. From a natural. Maybe he, Danny Morgan, was a natural when it came to art?

Why not?

"What a load of garbage," he suddenly muttered. "Ah, let me get out of here."

He turned abruptly away from the group and hurriedly walked through the galleries to the stairway and was about to descend, when he stopped, his hand on the smooth stone banister.

He would look at it again. Once more.

Maybe the illusion would vanish, and he would see it as it really was, the true lost Van Gogh. He went back through the galleries and came again to the painting. Came to it, and this time did not look at it, deliberately did not look at it, until he had taken a full, deep breath — just as he did sometimes during a football game, when he was about to carry the ball on a quarterback sneak, and he wanted to make sure that his nerves and his reflexes and his mind were all in tune.

Now he looked at the painting, slowly and steadily, and as he did, he felt a surge begin and roll over his entire being. It was a cry of triumph, of fierce angry triumph.

He was right. They were wrong. It was no illusion, but harsh, grim reality. The Antonellis had fallen and lay dead on the floor.

This was not the lost Van Gogh that had just been given back to the world. This was a lie. Now he was sure of it, the same as he was sure that he would always recognize and respond to George Cheever — because he knew and loved him as a human being. And he had come to love this painting as the expression of a good human being. There it was. Just as he would know George Cheever anywhere, even though somebody would try to make up like George, would even put on his face and skin and his eyes and his hands and his smile, even though he did everything, still Danny would know it was a lie. For at a glance he always recognized the sunniness that was in George, even when George was angry and gloomy. For this was George.

No one could fake that. The same way no one could fake the heartbreak that was in the very blood and bones of that Van Gogh. Deep within the stillness of the wheat caught in the violent storm was the heartbreak.

It seemed that Vincent Van Gogh was asking through the painting for an end of violence and evil in the world, was showing through his turbulent brushstrokes the heartbreak that comes from this violence and evil and was calling for a love of all people. The very way the stalks of wheat leaned one upon the other told him that — leaned in faith and peace, while the storm roared and raged about them.

That's what he had seen in the painting . . . had seen it the very first time. The very first time, when Walter Collingwood had made him really look at it. That's what he had seen in the painting. Deep within it. And no matter what anyone said, that was now all gone, gone.

Now he knew the truth. And the truth made him bitter. For he knew that a terrible crime had been committed, and he wondered whether he would walk away from it. Whether he could turn his back upon it all, leave the museum, and pick up things as before.

"Something the matter, son?"

Danny turned sharply and saw the twinkling eyes of the museum guard. The man's voice was low and concerned.

"The matter?"

"You lose something?"

Danny didn't speak. The discussion group had broken up, the individuals had moved off. Danny and the guard stood alone in a corner of the room, not far from the painting.

"Did you, son?" the man asked again.

He was small, bald-headed, and had clear, gentle features. His lips were soft and kind, ready to smile. Behind the twinkle of the blue eyes — they were a deep blue tending to black — Danny sensed a watchfulness, like that he once had seen behind the golden eyes of an alley tomcat, just before it sprang and ripped open a sparrow with one sweep of its paw.

"You look a bit ill."

This little guard with the gentle face knew everybody who came within a yard of the painting. Knew and appraised and remembered, and now he was appraising Danny.

"No," Danny said. "I didn't lose anything."

"And you feel all right?"

"Yes."

"You look a bit pale, son."

"I feel all right," Danny said.

"You go to school around here?"

He was like a policeman guarding a big payroll, wanting to know why anybody was on the same side of the street with him. From the corner of his eye Danny could see the guard from the next gallery standing still and watching them. He was a tall, dour-looking man with tight features and movements. Danny instinctively didn't like the man.

"Yes," Danny said. "One of my teachers is Mr. Warfield."

The man's eyes opened wide as Danny said the name.

"Warfield?"

"He says he knows you."

"Does he?"

Danny took the note out of his pocket, the note the teacher wanted signed, and handed it to the guard. He saw the man read it and begin to smile, then chuckle.

"So Bob Warfield doesn't trust you?"

"Just wanted you to sign it."

The little guard nodded kindly and sympathetically.

"I understand. I'll do that for you."

He took out a pencil from his inside pocket, and placed the note against the wall, and signed his name. Then he carefully folded the note and handed it to Danny. As Danny took the piece of paper, he noticed the dour guard still watching them.

"You didn't read it, did you, son?"

"No."

"Are you going to read it now?"

Danny shook his head.

"Tell Bob to read it to you when you give it to him."

Danny put the note back into his pocket silently. The little guard stood gazing up at him and then suddenly put his hand out.

"I'm Alfred Cobb. You're Daniel Morgan. So the note says."

"Yes."

Danny shook his hand. It was a small hand, but it had a strong grip, a grip that surprised Danny; he hadn't expected it. Then he remembered the watchful look behind the twinkle, and he knew that underneath it all he did expect it.

"How do you get along with Bob?"

"All right," Danny said. But he knew he wasn't fooling the man, for a soft smile was playing along the gentle lips.

"He can be a tough one when he wants to," Cobb said. "Tough and mean."

"You know him long?"

"We were in the Army together."

He put his small hand into his pants pocket and slowly drew out a crumpled white paper bag as he spoke. "Just take it easy with him. Do what he wants, and you'll have no trouble." He took out a piece of hard candy and then plumped it into his mouth. "No trouble. No trouble at all. Just don't rock the boat, son. Never rock the boat."

"The painting's a fake," Danny suddenly said, and the instant he did, he regretted it.

The man's mouth opened till Danny could see

the piece of red candy stuck on his tongue; then the mouth closed, and the piece of red hard candy disappeared.

"What?"

"Nothing," Danny said and wondered how he had come to reveal what was within him to this man.

Cobb looked at Danny's impassive face and began to laugh softly.

"I can see why you're having trouble with Bob Warfield. Why do you think the painting's false?"

"I didn't mean what I said."

"But you said it."

Danny shrugged.

"Let's get this straight. You're talking about the Van Gogh. This one over here."

The little guard motioned to the painting and the easel standing next to it. It was getting very near to closing time, and the room was now almost empty. A few persons lingered. The dour guard leaned against the archway of the next gallery and casually looked about him. He seemed to have lost interest in the two.

"This one here," Danny muttered.

"And you say it's a fake."

"Yes."

Cobb turned away from the painting and back to Danny. He stood staring at him, as if trying to make him out.

"What do you know about Van Gogh?" he suddenly asked as if he were a teacher questioning an unruly pupil.

"Nothing."

"You're being modest."

"Nothing," Danny repeated.

"I spent a lifetime studying him."

Danny was silent.

"What do you know about the French impressionists?"

Danny still kept silent.

"What do you know about Gauguin?"

"Ganguin?"

"Paul Gauguin, a contemporary of Van Gogh. A friend. He visited him at Arles. This painting was probably done at that time."

Cobb smiled at Danny and then said quietly: "So you know?"

"Nothing."

"I thought so."

"It's not Van Gogh," Danny said.

The shadows had begun to come into the high room.

"You like to rock a boat, don't you, son," Cobb said and began to laugh softly. "That's how you youngsters are today. Some of you anyway. Do anything for a little action. A thrill. It's the psychedelic age, isn't it? LSD equals STP and so on till you hit the next planet."

He took out another candy and plunked it into his mouth.

"You'd like to stir up a little trouble. A little interest. Make a little wave. Just for the hell of it. That's how you kids are."

He sucked on the candy a moment and then leaned forward to Danny.

"But I'm interested. Really interested why you

think this painting is not an authentic Van Gogh."

"Just don't think it is," Danny said.

"Think? You have doubts?"

"No doubts."

"That's what I thought. You young ones are always so sure of things. As if you created the world all by yourselves. Eh?"

Danny thought of walking away from the man and out of the museum. But he stood where he was and waited for him to speak again.

"Give me some reasons. You must have reasons."

"I was here on Saturday," Danny said.

"And?"

"This is not the painting that I saw here on Saturday."

For an instant Danny thought he saw the man tighten up. He wasn't sure of it. It could have been an illusion. It happened so fast — if it did happen.

"Oh," Cobb said, almost sighing out the word.

"It's not the same," Danny said grimly.

"I begin to understand."

He nodded his head slowly and studied Danny's face intently.

"So that's it," he murmured.

Then he swallowed the candy and pursed his soft lips thoughtfully. Suddenly the blue eyes began to twinkle again.

"Then what you are saying is this, Danny Morgan. That the painting you saw on Saturday was the Van Gogh."

"Yes."

"No question in your mind about that?"

"None."

"But something has happened between Saturday and now."

"Something has happened."

Cobb drew him closer to the painting. His voice became almost merry. His eyes danced.

"We have a puzzle on our hands, haven't we?"

He made a broad and expansive gesture with his little hand.

"A puzzle. This one is not the painting. And if it is not, why is it not?"

Danny looked away from Cobb's laughing eyes to the gray shadows that now lay in patterns over the room.

He heard Cobb's voice and turned.

"A puzzle. Why does everybody say it is Van Gogh when it is really not? Why?"

This time Cobb was laughing. He patted Danny on the arm.

"You have a wonderful imagination, Danny. Anybody ever tell you that? You should be a poet. You probably are one. You do write poetry, don't you, son?"

He laughed heartily and patted Danny again.

"No, son," he said with emphasis, the laughter beginning to die out of his voice. "This is the very same painting you saw on Saturday. This is the Van Gogh that was found in Arles just a little while ago and brought to this country."

He walked to within a few feet of the canvas and then motioned Danny to come to his side. Danny slowly, reluctantly did so.

"Let me show you, Danny, why you are wrong. Just stand by me and look with me."

Cobb smiled gently up at him, and Danny thought of Walter Collingwood doing the same with him on Saturday afternoon. Making him come to the canvas and look and see it come alive.

"Just one element of art. One and I'm sure I'll convince you. Do you see the yellow here in this little corner of the painting?"

He put his hand close to the canvas and cupped it like the eyeglass of a telescope.

"The top of the wheat stalk. I have my hand cupped about the top. Now look through it as you would through a glass. Look at the yellow."

Danny bent over and saw the yellow glow.

"The top of the wheat stalk," Cobb repeated. "Do you see it?"

He waited for Danny to nod.

"Good," he said with satisfaction. He smiled tenderly at Danny.

"That bit of yellow is what I call a Van Gogh color. No one in the history of painting has done a yellow like this. It is his and his alone. This holds with many painters, Danny. The great ones. The way they handle a particular color. You get to know them that way. It's their signature. No one else can do it. So no one can really fake them."

He paused and then said quietly, "No one could fool me on Van Gogh."

He shook his head definitely. "No one."

Danny was silent.

"I could go over this entire painting with you, square inch by square inch, and show you how without doubt this is authentic. The very same painting you saw here Saturday. The very same one, Danny."

And yet it is not, Danny wanted to say to him but didn't.

"It is Van Gogh," Cobb said.

The tall guard had come over to them.

"It's closing time, Al," he said to Cobb.

Cobb nodded.

"Okay, Smitty."

He turned to Danny with a smile.

"You'd better go, son. Give Bob Warfield my regards."

"I will."

Danny started to walk out of the room, and as he did he heard the tall guard say to Cobb:

"What were you telling the kid?"

When he had gone through the succession of galleries, he looked back. There, against the archway, he saw the figure of the tall guard; the tight face looked grimly through the darkening space at him.

11

Clear through the wood of the closed door, he heard the ring of the telephone. Again and again. Finally, he got out of bed and opened the door and went down the hallway to the telephone. When he got to it, the ringing had stopped. He stood there in the darkness and silence of the hall, and then slowly went back to his room and closed the door and went to bed.

A little later in the night he heard the ring again. This time when he got to the phone and picked up the receiver he heard someone breathing softly on the other end, but there was no answer to his hello. . . .

Hello . . .

No answer.

Then he heard the receiver slowly set onto the hook and the dial tone rush in. He stood there and suddenly wanted to speak to his mother, but she was not home yet.

He went back to his room and sat on his bed in the darkness and found himself waiting for the phone to ring again.

When it did and he picked up the receiver, he

*heard a voice that he had never heard before. A
slow, even voice with iron in it.*
"Don't rock the boat, Danny."
That was all.
*The click and the dial tone and then the silence
all about him.*

"It was a good report, Morgan."

They sat alone in the classroom, the teacher
and the pupil.

"Thank you, Mr. Warfield."

Danny's voice was polite but distant. The
teacher didn't seem to be aware of it.

"Shows a fine appreciation of Van Gogh. I'm
very pleased. Even excited."

He looked across his desk to Danny and
smiled.

"I only kept you after class to tell you how
pleased I am. I think I owe that to you."

Danny was silent.

"I hope you understand why I was rough with
you."

"Yes," Danny said.

Outside it was cold, the gray of winter was
over the street.

Suddenly, during the day, while Danny sat in
his class and thought of the ring of the phone and
heard again the voice, while he sat there and
gazed at the rugged, harsh figure of Mr. Warfield
and tried to fathom him, while he was in the
midst of all this, his eyes sought the window, as
if by a signal, and saw immediately the first strike
of winter.

Then he looked across the row of heads till he found George Cheever, and his dark sunny face and aware eyes. George nodded. He too knew that winter had suddenly come. Danny remembered their sitting in the park and George's saying that it would be a tough winter. Lots of snow and ice. And fear, Danny added grimly.

"But sometimes a teacher has to take harsh measures. Just has to. I think I was justified. Don't you, Morgan?"

Danny forced himself back to the reality of the teacher.

"Yes, Mr. Warfield," he said.

Mr. Warfield smiled and leaned forward.

"I'd like to be your friend, Morgan," he said.

And at that instant, that very instant, Danny's fingers felt the note that still lay in his jacket pocket, felt it, and became aware of it. He had forgotten the note, and Mr. Warfield had not asked for it.

Friends? Danny thought.

"Mr. Warfield, the report that you like so much and that excites you was the one I left home. The one you claimed I never wrote," he said bitterly. "You called me a liar. You didn't believe I had gone to the museum on Saturday. You even had me take a note to the guard, like a little kindergarten kid."

Mr. Warfield's face had paled.

"Then you did see the painting on Saturday," he said quietly.

"Saturday."

"I believe you now."

"Why was it so important to you that I went on Saturday and not Monday?"

"What?"

He seemed to have caught the man off guard.

"Why? Why?" Danny almost shouted.

He took the note out and grimly handed it to the teacher.

"You forgot about the note, didn't you, Mr. Warfield?"

"I did."

"Do you mind reading it to me? The guard said you should read it to me."

Mr. Warfield held the note in his rugged hand. A slip of white folded paper against the tanned, vigorous skin. The hand tightened into a fist and crumpled the white paper, then threw it into the wastebasket.

"I wrote it in anger. It's best forgotten."

"What did you write?"

"Best forgotten, Morgan," the teacher said.

"Why?"

Mr. Warfield did not answer.

"What did the guard write?"

"The guard?"

"Alfred Cobb. He said he knew you from Army days."

"That is true."

"What did he write?"

"Morgan, you seem to be putting me on a witness stand."

"Maybe I have a right to."

"A right?"

"Yes."

"Don't you think you're going a bit too far?" the teacher said, his voice hardening.

"No."

Mr. Warfield looked long at Danny and then sighed out: "I'm sorry for being harsh with you. For not believing you." His jaw muscles quivered. "You have my apology, Morgan."

Danny was silent.

Mr. Warfield put his hand out to him.

"Can we be friends?"

"No," Danny said.

And without asking the teacher's permission, he got up and walked out of the room.

12

But when he had walked up the corridor but a few steps, something told him to turn and go back, some hidden sense that he had developed from his playing football, and so he turned and went back and looked through the glass panel of the door and saw Mr. Warfield straightening up from the wastebasket, holding the note in his scarred hand. He read it, his face darkening to a deep wine color, then he savagely tore it into tiny bits and let the bits flutter back into the waste-basket . . .

13

*. . . flutter back into the wastebasket like the
snow that started to fall as Danny walked into the
park on his way home.*

The day had not yet begun its swift slide into
night, and the sky was iron gray, white flecks of
snow falling out of it and down onto the bare
branches of the trees.

He walked along slowly, thinking deeply and
worriedly about what was happening to him. Trying to understand it, and to find his way through.
He felt that he should talk to someone — to Carol
or George — but at the same time he knew that
he wouldn't, that he would follow the pattern of
his life and work things out for himself. It was always that way with him. It always would be.

Once a loner, always a loner.

He smiled bitterly and brushed his wet, snowy
hair back with his hand and then buttoned the
top button of his overcoat. He thought of his
mother and his argument with her over the job
at the drugstore. He wanted it so he could earn
some money for a new coat. So she shouldn't

have to use her money for him. It all seemed so remote, so distant, so meaningless now.

He let the snow fall on his raised hand, palm upward, and watched the flakes drop and dissolve and become things of nothing. Right before his eyes. Nothing, nothingness. It was snow, and now it was water dripping over his palm, and when the water dried up, it was as if it had never existed.

What was illusion and what was reality?

Did the Antonellis really fall when he saw them fall or when his father and all the others in the vast crowd saw them?

Illusion.

Reality.

First you see a painting and then you don't.

The lost Van Gogh is lost again.

That's what *I* say.

Don't rock the boat.

Danny shrugged, a grim, twisted look on his face, and slowly sat down on a bench. He knew this old bench and loved sitting on it. It stood just where the lake curved and then began to narrow. From where he sat, Danny could see clear across the water to the other side, to the hill that gently sloped upward till it seemed to disappear into the grayness of the low sky.

He had climbed that hill many times. In winter and summer, at night and at day. He had gone up to its crest with Carol and sat with her in the sun, watching it glint off her honeyblonde hair like sparks.

Danny suddenly felt a longing to have her at

his side now. She would sit with him in the gently falling snow, sit and drive away his loneness.

He shrugged again.

A lamppost stood a little away from the bench, an old iron green-painted lamppost. Unlighted, it looked lonely and forlorn, as if it waited for its light to go on and give it reason and being.

It cast a thin shadow. Danny sat and looked out over the snow falling into the water, when he heard the sound of a cane, muffled when it hit a layer of snow and harsh when it hit the pavement. It slowly approached and then stopped.

Dead.

When he looked up, he saw the long, taut figure of Mr. Collingwood standing over him.

"Hello, Danny."

The snow fell quietly, muffling all sounds but the voice of the man who stood tall and studied the youth with impassive eyes.

"You're surprised to see me."

Danny slowly nodded.

"Do you mind if I sit with you awhile?"

"No."

He sat down and leaned his cane at his side. He wore a long, dark overcoat that was now getting white with snow. On his head was a coal-black felt hat with its brim turned down. It, too, was getting powdered with snow.

"It will soon be night," the lean man said.

Danny kept looking at the snow slanting into the lake, looking at its relentless flakes and waiting.

The flat voice began again. "As you see, I

didn't go back to Seattle." A pause. "I've had a change of plans. A slight change of plans."

The "slight" was softly emphasized.

Across the lake on the slope of the hill a few figures started to move — blurred figures which scrambled upward, upward into the darkening sky. Some kids, Danny thought, having their last fling of fun in the snow before the night came down hard and swept them out of the park. And into their snug and safe homes.

Danny watched them till they finally disappeared over the crest of the hill. The slope was quiet and alone again. All he could see now was the bare branches of the trees that straggled upward. Like gaunt scarecrows.

"The painting is a fake, Danny."

Danny turned and looked at Collingwood. A thin smile hovered on the man's face. He slowly nodded.

"You were right. The true Van Gogh is gone."

Silence.

"You saw it at once, didn't you?"

The brim of the black felt hat shadowed the narrow face. The thin lips gleamed and moved again.

"You and you alone. A mere boy."

The man laughed softly. "A boy saw that the emperor was naked."

He paused and rested his hand on his cane. "You, of course, know Hans Andersen's fairy tale, don't you?"

When Danny didn't answer, he laughed again. It was a flat, almost harsh laugh.

"A child cries out the truth, and no one sees

it. No one. It's all a cosmic jest." His voice became bleak. "But it is the bitter reality."

His hand gripped the solid cane, and he was silent. His head bent forward, peering grimly into the oncoming darkness.

"A jest." Danny barely heard him say.

The words seemed to whisper into the whirling air and away. To whisper and then to echo sibilantly.

"A jesssssssst."

Danny felt the man laughing soundlessly.

Suddenly across the lake a light went on, the light of a distant lamppost. It shivered through the falling snow and onto the water in a flat, golden streak. But the lamppost that stood near them was still lightless.

A stillness lay over the entire park. The white snow had choked away all sounds. Then the man's voice edged through the silence.

"Danny, do you know the story of Cain and Abel?"

Danny didn't speak.

Just over the crest of the hill on the other side, a blotch of lambent red, as from a fierce fire, spread over the sky, and as it appeared, almost at the very moment, it started just as quickly and suddenly to fade out, from red into pink, into rose, and then into black nothingness.

"It is a story of death."

It is, Danny thought.

"And out of this story of death comes one of the world's immortal lines. Do you know the line I mean?"

"No," Danny said, but he knew.

109

"Then I shall tell you."

The man's lean and tapering finger tapped on Danny's knee as he spoke. "It is: Am I my brother's keeper?"

The finger paused. "Illusion tells us to say yes, we are. But harsh, grim reality tells us to say no."

Now the light on the lamppost near their bench suddenly came into being. But its arc did not reach entirely to them, so they sat on the bench, half in shining light and half in darkness.

The man was more in darkness than the boy.

"You are not your brother's keeper, Danny. It is enough to take care of yourself in this savage world, isn't it?"

The man's eyes gleamed like a bird's in the darkness. "You lost a father to death. Isn't that enough?"

"You know all about me, don't you?" Danny spoke bitterly and desperately.

"Yes, Danny. All that I need to know."

Danny leaned forward to him. "Who are you, Mr. Collingwood? Who?"

"Just a man who loves art as you do."

Danny shook his head. "You've never come from Seattle," he said. "Never."

"That could be true."

"Where do you come from?"

"Does it matter, Danny?"

The snow fell silently between them. Like a long curtain.

"What do you want of me?" the boy suddenly asked.

"Nothing."

But within, deep within, Danny knew that before it all ended the man sitting in the darkness would want his life.

"Nothing," Mr. Collingwood said. "Just that you go on as before."

"As before?"

"You saw nothing. You know nothing. You say nothing."

"I've already told the guard."

"We know that."

Danny was silent.

"You've told no one else."

"No one."

"Good."

Danny thought he could see a smile flicker on the man's lips.

"No one would believe me anyway," Danny said.

"True. But just the same it's dangerous to speak." There was a pause. "The painting is worth over half a million dollars, Danny."

"Half a million?"

"I'm with violent people, Danny. Hard to control when it comes to half a million dollars in cash. That is why I ask you to keep out of this."

"Who wanted to be in it anyway?" Danny said fiercely.

"Sometimes life doesn't seem to care about what we want, Danny. When you get older you'll understand that better."

Will I get older? Danny thought, looking at the man.

"I came to your house the other night and sat in my car and looked up to your window. Thinking. Just thinking. In the dead of night, sitting there and thinking. Why did I make you look at the Van Gogh? Why did I talk to you? Why did I do it? Why didn't I just let you turn and go out of the museum? Why? What possessed me?" His voice rose against the night. "What?" Then he said low and grim, his eyes smoldering, "We never do what we want to do. We are driven."

With his hand he brushed away the snow from his coat. Fierce, long strokes.

"Driven. Just as I was driven to steal the Van Gogh. The instant I heard of it. The instant I first saw it in France, where it was shown for a few days, I was driven. For money?" He laughed almost bitterly. "For love, Danny. I love art as you do. I once taught it. Then I got tired of teaching. Tired of writing about art. I wanted to possess it. But what I wanted I could not buy. So I started stealing what I wanted. Some I kept and some I sold." He turned away from the boy and said almost like a litany. "Some I keep and some I sell. Some I keep and some I sell. While on the way, I go to hell." He turned back to the boy. "What should I do with the Van Gogh, Danny? Keep or sell?"

When the boy didn't answer, he laughed hard.

"To steal the Van Gogh I needed help. It was too big a job for me. I needed people who steal for money. And money alone." He smiled sardonically. "They are not like us, Danny. They look at a painting and see dollar bills. You and I see the soul of a man."

He shook his head.

"But this time you can have the soul. I will take the money. We have a buyer in France. He has already deposited a hundred thousand dollars in a Swiss bank as a down payment for the painting. For the real Van Gogh."

The man's thin nostrils quivered and then he went on.

"We have the real Van Gogh. But we need time to deliver it safely to our buyer. A little time. That is all we need now."

The man rose to his full height.

"You alone know the truth. Keep it that way." Danny rose.

"Someone will find it out. Sooner or later," he said.

Collingwood shook his head.

"Later, maybe. The copy that is now in the museum is perfect. Only scientific tests would tell that it is a fraud. But by that time it wouldn't matter. We'd be gone from this continent, the money in our pockets."

He moved a few paces off and then turned and held out his cane and touched Danny with it lightly. A shudder went through the boy as he felt the point of the cane against him.

"We need only a few days, Danny. Make sure you give it to us."

He tapped the cane against Danny's chest for emphasis.

"By silence."

Then he turned and disappeared in the snowy night.

14

The snow fell silently for two hours, and then it stopped. Just as silently. He was lying on his bed in the dark of the room, and he didn't know when it stopped. He was lying there, his clothes still on, lying there thinking, ever thinking.

Am I my brother's keeper?

Then when his mind became tired of that, he remembered the lean man's bleak words against the falling snow.

Haven't you lost enough to death?

He could see the dark brim shading the birdlike eyes. He could see the glimmer of light on the thin lips as they moved soundlessly.

Haven't you lost enough to death?

Lips moving soundlessly but continuously.

You lost a father. Isn't that enough?

Then the images faded out, and he was alone in silence. He lay on his back, his legs sprawled out, his eyes staring up into the darkness, and suddenly he realized without going to the window and raising the shade to look out that the snow had stopped. That all was silent. Completely silent. In the house and outside on the snow-muffled street. It was then that the words and the melody of "Deathman, Do Not Follow Me," came into his mind and seemed to float about him in the dark. And as they did he could see the black hat, the coal-black hat shimmering.

Deathman, do not follow me
Be you good, be you evil,
Deathman, Deathman,
Do not follow me.

Suddenly for the first time in years he felt like crying.

"Danny?"

It was his mother's voice on the other side of the door.

He didn't answer.

"Danny, are you in there?"

Still he couldn't answer.

"Danny?"

This time she opened the door and came in. She stopped just past the threshold, her voice dying out.

"Why are you lying in the dark?"

"Resting," he said in a low voice.

The light of the hallway outlined her lithe figure. She still had her hat and coat on, and they were wet and glistening. Her eyes seemed bright to him, as if she had just come in from a walk with someone she liked. But the rest of her was pale and anxious.

"Have you had supper yet?"

"No."

"Why not?"

"Just wasn't hungry."

"You always have supper. Whether I'm home or not."

He didn't speak.

"Shall I make you something?"

"No."

She came in to him.

"Aren't you feeling well, Danny?"

He slowly sat up.

"I'm all right."

"Are you sure?"

"Sure."

"You don't sound it."

"How am I supposed to sound?"

"You're not well," she said.

He swung off the bed and stood up. She saw the haggard look on his face as the light hit it. She put her hand to his cheek tentatively. Her touch was cold to him, and he flinched away from it.

"I told you I'm all right," he said gruffly.

"Just wanted to see if you had fever."

"Cut it, Mom. Please."

He walked past her and through the narrow hallway to the kitchen. The lighted room swept against his eyes, and he raised his hand as if to ward off a blow. Then he sat down at the kitchen table.

"I'll make you some hot soup," she said.

He felt her standing behind him, studying him very closely.

"Okay."

While she warmed the soup, they didn't speak. Once when the soup started to bubble and boil and the cozy sound came into the room and reminded him of the warm winter nights sitting there with his father and mother, all eating quietly, he wanted to blurt out to her:

Help me. Tell me what to do.

But he didn't say anything to her.

She set the two plates on the table, cut some bread, and then sat down across from him. Two ribbons of steam rose from the two plates.

"It's hot," she said.

"Looks it."

"But it's good for you."

"Guess it is."

"How does it taste?"

"Fine."

"Sip it."

"I am."

"Till it cools," she smiled.

"Seems like it never will," he smiled.

"It will."

"Okay."

He took a piece of bread and slowly buttered it. Through the kitchen window he could see the roofs spread away from him, white with snow against a cloudless night.

The act of eating, of sitting across the table from her, was bringing him nearer to her again. He felt that soon he would speak to her and tell her of what was happening to him, and then the telephone rang.

They looked silently at each other; Danny got up and went into the hallway to the phone.

"Hello?"

"Hello, Danny."

It was George Cheever.

"How are you, man?"

"Okay, George."

"You don't sound it."

Danny shrugged silently. The ring of the telephone had chilled him. But now hearing George's voice, he felt the chill going away. Slowly going away.

"It's a great night for skating. How about it?"

"Not in the mood."

"Great for the wind, for the muscles, Danny. The leg muscles."

"I know."

"Something is bugging you. What is it?"

"Nothing."

"Then come on. It's a clear night, Danny. A real clear night. The kind of night you always like."

Danny hesitated.

"I'll meet you at the rink in an hour. Give you enough time. What do you say?"

"I don't know, George."

"Buck up, man. It's winter, and the stars will soon be out singing."

The voice was resonant and sunny. George Cheever's hello-to-life voice. The voice that came from the house where there were shouts and laughter and angry tears. It made him think of the painting. And he didn't know why, but this time when he thought of it, he could see it and feel it and feel good. As though the painting were still where it rightfully belonged, in a museum where people could see it and enjoy it, and no rotten crooks had stolen it away for themselves and the money it could bring. The painting was still there and not a fake and a lie that was put in its place to fool the people.

"Get hold of Carol and bring her along. I'll bring Loretta Stokes."

"Loretta? She can't skate."

"That's why I'm bringing her. I'll have my arm about her all the time. So what do you say?"

Danny hesitated.

"Well?"

"Let me think it over."

"No thinking time left. So signals on, and let's go," George barked out like a quarterback. "Give me the ball, and let's hit that line."

"I'll call you back in ten minutes. I'm eating."

"No. Let me call you."

"Okay."

"So long, Danny."

"So long, George."

He heard the lusty bang of the phone on the other end and almost chuckled. When he got back to the kitchen, his eyes were smiling.

"It was George," he said to his mother.

"What did he want?"

"Go skating. In the park rink."

"Do you think you should?"

He took another piece of bread and buttered it slowly and methodically.

"Maybe I'll go, and maybe I won't. I'll see how I feel."

In a little while the phone rang again. He didn't seem to hear it. His mother looked across the table at him and then rose and went to it. She soon came back into the room.

"It's Carol."

His eyes lighted up, and he went into the hall-way thinking of the girl and of the way she some-times walked with him, her arm linked in his.

"Hello, Carol."

Then he sat back and listened to her speak.

"George just called me," she said.

"Oh."

He never realized how pleasant and soothing it was just listening to her speak.

"How about it, Danny?"

"Don't know."

"What's there to know? Get your skates ready and start moving."

"This a command?"

"How'd you guess it?"

He just smiled and didn't answer.

"Make it in a half hour. In front of the rink."

"Half hour?"

"Synchronize your watch."

"It is."

"It is what?"

"Always synchronized to your watch."

She laughed, and he sat with the phone close to his ear listening till the rippling laughter was gone, completely gone.

"I'll call George and tell him you'll meet us."

"If you want."

"I do."

"Then do it."

"Cool it, man," she said.

"Cool it, man," he said.

He sat there, long after he had heard the click of the receiver; then he went in and finished his

120

supper with a light, almost gay feeling. When he was about to leave, his skates slung over his shoulder, his mother said:

"You seem to be in good spirits, Danny."

"Just didn't feel right for awhile, Mom," he said.

"Have a good time."

"I will."

And he did have a good time, one of the best he ever had. It was only when the night was almost over, the skating rink about to be cleared that he saw the two figures standing in the gloom.

It was Mr. Warfield and the tall dour guard who was called Smitty.

They stood together, under a huge and desolate oak tree, their eyes on the darkening rink. Then, when the last overhead light dimmed out, they separated and walked off into the chilled night.

"Anything wrong, Danny?"

"What?"

"You look all pale."

And he knew that she hadn't seen the grim figures.

"Got a chill, that's all."

Later, after he left Carol and began to walk home, he felt that someone was following him. He was sure he heard the tapping of the cane.

But when he turned to look, there was nothing. Only the white streets and the night.

Suddenly he felt like screaming.

15

But he didn't scream.
It was only when he was home and in bed and
finally asleep and dreaming that he screamed.
But the door was closed, as he always kept it,
and his mother didn't hear him.
When he woke in the morning, his mother had
already left, so he was alone in the house when
the phone rang. He sat up in bed, listening to the
sound, till silence came in and throttled it. Then
he went forward and into the hallway and stood
there looking at the black phone with the thin
ray of sun gliding along it.
He knew that it was going to ring again.
Insistently.
But just as he was about to let go of the thought,
it rang.

Danny picked up the receiver, his hand
clammy.

"Hello?"

"Danny? Danny Morgan?"

It was a woman's voice. Instantly he recognized it. Somehow he was not surprised. Some-

how, deep within him, he had expected her to call.

"It's Danny," he said.

"I need your help. I can't speak too long."

"Yes?"

"I must see you this morning."

He was silent.

"Within the hour. I can't get away for longer."

And suddenly before him he could see the face of the woman. The side of the face with the agonizing scar that ran from ear to chin.

"Please."

"I'm being followed," he said. "Wherever I go."

"Meet me. No one will know. I can arrange it that way."

And now he saw the man standing beside her, with his lean hand closing about the end of the knobby cane.

"Why do you want me? What can I do?"

"I'll explain when I see you."

"I'm keeping my mouth shut. So what do they want from me?"

"Meet me. I'm only a short distance away."

"Let them do what they want with the painting. I don't care. Just let them leave me alone."

"Help me, and they will leave you alone."

"How?"

"Meet me in the library on Eastern Parkway. I'm near it now."

"The main one?"

"Yes."

He loved the big yet gentle building that overlooked the end of the park. He had spent countless hours roaming through it and studying there with his friends. But now he found himself fearing it.

"Take your books with you as if you're going there for school research. Be there in twenty minutes. Hurry."

Before he could speak again, she was gone.

He stood there, ringed about by silence. Then he went back to his room and slowly dressed, his fingers trembling as he buttoned his shirt.

The sun was brilliant on the snow as he walked up the steps of the library building. He paused at the top and looked down at the plaza. The cars were moving around the huge arch and into the park and up Eastern Parkway, a relentless, dark flow. The sky was clear and bright.

When he went inside and into the main hall, he saw her standing near the rows of the catalog files. Her hair was sleek, her face clean and beautiful. She turned and went into the room where the juvenile literature was kept. He waited and then followed her in.

He saw her take a few books from the shelves and then go to one of the far tables and sit down. Danny glanced about the room; aside from the librarian, there was no one else there at that early hour. He went over and sat down across the table from her. He opened his *World History* and started to make notes in his looseleaf book. She read. Neither paid any attention to the other.

When she spoke, her voice was low, very low, but very clear.

"We haven't much time to talk. I must leave here very soon."

He glanced across the table at her.

"Keep writing while I speak," she said. "Show no emotion. Just sit there and listen. But listen closely."

He began writing again.

"For the while we are both safe. But only for the while. That is why I did what I did." She paused and then went on. Her voice became even lower, melodic, and urgent.

"Danny, I've stolen the painting from Collingwood and the others."

"What?"

"Don't look up. Listen. I've done it to save him and you and me. If I let this go on, we would all be destroyed. All of us."

This time he did look up, and he saw her eyes. They were large and luminous.

"I was against this from the beginning. I told Collingwood it would not work, that it was too dangerous. Much, much too dangerous. That before it was over, there would be murder. There has to be, Danny. That is the way it's going. And I'm terrified."

She paused again. Her head was turned away from him, and he could see the line of the scar, bright red in the sunlight coming through the window.

"I love him, Danny," she said. "We've been together many years. He's a strange man. There is much that is good in him. So much that is fine

and esthetic. And there is so much that is dis-
torted. And cruel. Do you understand?"

Danny silently nodded.

"Yes, you do understand. You do."

Her small finger unconsciously moved along
the scar.

"He can be very cruel," she said. "He can hurt.
Terribly."

Moved along and stopped.

"But a woman in love excuses anything in a
man. If she is in love." Then she added gently, "A
woman in love is a very, very foolish woman,
Danny. She gives up a way of life that is hers
and takes on another one that is not hers. You
understand that too, don't you?"

She was now looking fully at him. A gentle,
sad smile came into her eyes.

"There is so much in you that is old, Danny.
You are so far ahead of yourself in some respects.
I could talk to you as I talk to him and feel no
difference. I feel as though I've known you for
years."

"For years," Danny murmured.

"And he feels the same. He has said that to
me. That is the strangeness and the mystery of
it all. He said to me, 'Of all the people in the
world, the boy had to discover the truth. The
boy.' "

She sighed. "We could have been great friends.
Couldn't we, Danny?"

And she repeated it. "Couldn't we, Danny?"
Then she was silent.

He waited for her to speak again, and while

he did, he stared at the meaningless words he had scribbled on the white, lined paper.

"Collingwood is a thief," she said. "And so am I. But up to this time we went along without death at our side. We have been all over the world, Danny. We have made our way. We have never been caught before. Never."

The words on the page shimmered as he heard her say that.

"Until now. This time, he's got himself mixed up with deadly people. This is what I've begun to fear. For the first time we have the smell of death. Do you know what I mean, Danny?"

Danny saw the tears glisten in her eyes.

"If you tried to betray them, they would kill you, Danny. Or anybody dear to you. Anybody."

"I knew that from the beginning," Danny said in a low, dull voice.

"And even if you didn't betray them . . ."

Her voice trailed off.

"I couldn't let that happen to you," she said. "I couldn't. Where there is no painting to be sold, there is no longer any cause for death. That is why I stole it and hid it away."

"But they'll soon find out."

"If they haven't already," she said grimly. "But they'll never know where it's hidden."

"What will happen to you?"

"I'm going to the airport from here, Danny. And out of the country. I'll manage."

"Collingwood?"

"After awhile I'll let him know where I am. We'll be together again. It will work out."

Will it? he thought. But he didn't say anything, for there was a glow in her eyes. A glow of hope and triumph. It made him feel sad for her.

She leaned forward and spoke almost in a whisper.

"The painting has been checked at Penn Station. I've destroyed the ticket. Write down the number. Six-eight-seven-three-four."

She repeated the number as he wrote it. Then he took the slip of paper and put it carefully in his wallet, while she watched approvingly.

"Memorize it and then tear up the paper. Wait a week and then go to the police and have them claim the package."

"The police?"

"Yes. By that time Collingwood and the rest will be gone. So do what I say."

She got up.

"What has Mr. Warfield to do with it all?" he suddenly asked.

"Warfield?"

"My teacher."

She shook her head.

"Trust nobody. Speak to nobody. Just do as I said. Good-bye and God keep you."

She was about to go when she turned and came slowly back to him.

"You have a girl, don't you?"

"Yes."

"Then you know what it means to care for someone."

"I know," he said.

This time she went away without a word.

He watched her walk out of the room. He waited awhile and then got up and went out and into the sunshine. He stood on the peak of the stone steps and looked down across the plaza, and there he could see her walking briskly along the snowy sidewalk. And as she walked, he suddenly noticed the black limousine that began slowly following her. Then it drew up beside her, and a man got out and tried to drag her into the car. She broke loose and began to run across the wide plaza, a small figure with another figure after it, and as she ran, he knew, before the truck bearing down upon her hit her, that she was marked for death.

He heard the scream float up, up to him and the screeching of the anguished brakes, and he heard the silence. Then he saw the black limousine streak away and disappear among the bare trees of Prospect Park.

16

He pushed his way through the growing cluster of people till he got to her side. She was still alive. He sat down in the snowy street and let her rest against him. She looked up at him and said nothing. But he knew what was in her heart, for it was in his, too.

"Why are we all so cruel to each other?" she said.

By the time the ambulance came, she was dead.

17

He walked aimlessly about, still hearing her scream float up to him. There were now tears on his face, and he didn't know what he was crying for, but it was for something lost that he would never find again. Never.

We could have been great friends, Danny. Couldn't we? She was stiting across the table from him, the sun gleaming through the library window, falling upon her, making her eyes glow. Couldn't we?

He wiped the tears from his face with a sweep of his hand. He suddenly felt a fierce hatred for Collingwood and all the rest of them. He took out the piece of paper from his wallet and stared at the number, stared at it till it burned itself into his memory, then he tore the paper up into little bits and watched the wind carry them away over the desolate street.

The hell with them all now. They would never get the painting as long as he lived.

As long as he lived.

And the words repeated became words of fear. His legs trembled. He leaned back against the bars of an iron fence and looked up into the sky.

It had turned gray and ready for snow.
As long as he lived.
He tried to fight the wave of fear that now went over him again and again. His hands gripped the bars, and as they did, he realized that the fence was the one that surrounded his school building.

"Hello, Danny."

The rugged figure of Mr. Warfield stood before him, eyes piercing into Danny's. The two stood alone on the windy street. Danny slowly let his fingers loosen from around the wet bars.

"What's wrong, Danny?"

"Wrong?"

"I've been watching you from the window."

"You've been watching me from every window," Danny said bitterly.

The teacher stood there without a jacket on, in his white shirt, and said nothing. Danny wiped his wet hands on his coat.

"You and Collingwood," he said.

"Collingwood?"

"Your friend, the murderer."

The teacher grabbed Danny by the arm, his eyes anxiously looking into the boy, trying to search him out.

"Danny, what are you talking about?"

"I see now why I came here. I came for help. From you, of all people."

"Help? From what, Danny?"

"Underneath it all I still believed in you. Still. You're a teacher. My friend." And then he almost shouted: "My friend the killer."

"Danny."

Danny flung himself loose from the iron grip.

"When did you first become a murderer?" he asked fiercely. "Was it in the war that you started? Was it then that you learned to kill?"

And when the man didn't speak, Danny asked the question again.

"When?"

"Danny. Danny, listen to me. I want to help you. Tell me what's wrong. All. I must know it all."

"Never," Danny said.

"Please."

He raised his hand in a pleading gesture, and as he did, the scar near the thumb stood clear. Instantly Danny saw the woman lying in the street, and the scar that ran from her ear to her chin.

"Did you hurt her, too?" he asked.

"Her?"

"Mrs. Collingwood. She's lying on the street dead."

The man's face blanched.

"Dead?"

"Who ripped that scar on her face? Was it you? Collingwood? Smitty? What animal hurt her so?"

Danny's voice almost broke, and he turned away.

"Danny. Danny, what are you talking about? Tell me, boy. Tell me."

"You know nothing."

"Nothing."

Danny turned to him.

"Liar."

The snow started to fall, in light grim strokes.

"When have I lied to you? When?"

"When didn't you lie to me?" Danny said.

And as he saw the agonized, searching look in the man's face, he thought bitterly of illusion and reality. How underneath that agonized look was evil. Bloody, monstrous evil.

"You are all alike," he said. "You and the Collingwoods of this world. All of you. You fool us. All the time. There isn't a minute when you're not fooling us."

He shook his head grimly. "But you won't win. Not even this time. You'll never get the painting. Tell that to Collingwood. And to your thieving friends at the museum."

He suddenly turned.

"Where are you going?"

"What's it your business?"

"Come inside. I want to talk to you more."

"No."

"Danny."

"I'm going to the police."

"Come inside."

The teacher reached forward to grab him, but Danny feinted away and then turned and ran. And as he ran, he heard the teacher calling after him:

"Danny . . . Danny . . . Dan . . . nn . . . y."

Till the voice was lost in the wind and the snow.

18

The snow kept falling from a smoky sky. He
paused at the end of a block and waited to cross.
From where he stood he could see the green light
of the police station faintly glimmering. It was
then that the black limousine stole up through
the mists and paused at his side, and he saw the
muzzle of the gun pointed straight at him. Then
the door opened, and he silently went into the
car. And as he did, a moist handkerchief was
thrust against his nostrils.
He soon lost consciousness.

19

He thought of birds, of soaring wings, of tall trees, and then the reflection of all on the cool, placid waters of the lake. Then he felt his father standing beside him, pointing out the different trees and the beauty of light as it struck an uplifted wing. He listened to the voice of his father till it got louder and louder, and he opened his eyes and saw Collingwood standing over him, lean and grim. Speaking through thinned lips.

"Sit up. Do as I say."
The man's voice was like a whiplash.
"Do it."
Behind Collingwood stood the small museum guard, Alfred Cobb, and a little beyond him, in the shadows of the room, was a heavyset man — the chauffeur of the black limousine.
"We haven't much time to waste on you," Collingwood said.
The room was large and dimly lighted. There were glass doors at one end that led out to a terrace that was now in darkness. Beyond a rail-

ing Danny could see the distant lights of the Verrazano Bridge. Distant and winking in the falling snow.

"We haven't much time. Or patience."

Collingwood stepped a bit closer to Danny. "You know what we want."

He loomed over the youth. On the sofa behind him, the knobby cane glinted. "Tell me."

Danny looked to the other men. Their faces were hard, their eyes bright.

"The painting. Where is it?"

"I don't know."

"She told you. We know she did."

Danny was silent.

"You're wasting time," the heavyset man said, and in his hand was a gun butt.

Collingwood turned sharply to him.

"I'll handle this."

"Let me give it to him with this gun butt. He'll talk."

"I said I'll handle it."

"Get it out of him."

"I will."

"Fast."

The man slowly stepped back into the shadows. Danny looked fearfully away from him, to the hard eyes of the museum guard and then back to Collingwood.

Out on the terrace the snow fell relentlessly.

"It's no use," Collingwood said. "You'd better tell us where it is."

"I can't."

"Why?"

"Because I don't know."

The man's thin nostrils quivered in fury.

"Liar."

He turned and grabbed up the cane.

"Where is it?"

Then Danny felt the hard blow across his legs and the flash of pain that ran through him.

He cried out low.

"Where?"

Collingwood waited and then struck again, this time across the chest.

"Fool!"

Danny went down to his knees and then stared up at the blazing eyes and the raised cane.

"Tell me!"

The cane hit Danny a slashing blow across the face, and he felt the blood, the hot salt blood, stream onto his lips.

"I can't," Danny said.

Collingwood was about to strike again, but he stepped back and slowly lowered his arm. He sat heavily on the sofa and stared down at the boy. A weary, agonized look came into his eyes.

"Why?" he asked. "Why?"

Danny knelt on the floor and dazedly wiped the blood from his lips and chin. His whole being ached with fear and pain.

"Why?" Collingwood almost shouted. "What have you to gain from this? What?"

"Nothing," Danny muttered. "Nothing.'"

"Then why don't you tell me?"

And when the boy didn't answer, he spoke again, but this time his voice seemed to break.

"Haven't I lost enough?" he said. "You saw her die. I've nothing left but this. Give me the painting. Give it to me."

To sell for money, Danny thought bitterly.

"You saw her. Look at the price I paid. It's mine. Danny, it's mine now. Why do you keep it from me? Why?"

Then he said again in a low, tortured voice, "You saw her die."

"We'll give you twenty grand," the museum guard said.

Collingwood sat on the sofa, breathing heavily, still staring down at Danny. The guard came closer.

"Thirty grand. No tricks, kid. You'll get the money. Hard cash."

He leaned over and wiped some of the blood from Danny's lips with a large handkerchief.

"What more do you want, kid? It'll be all yours. To do with as you like. All yours."

"I'll beat him to death if he don't talk," the heavyset man said, and he was now standing over Danny, the gun butt gripped in his hand.

Collingwood rose and fiercely motioned the two away. Then he spoke to Danny, softly.

"If you take the money, you'll walk out of here alive."

Danny thought of the woman lying in the street, her face in the muddy snow, and he could not speak again.

"Why should we have to kill you, boy? Why?"

Then he leaned on the cane and thrust his face close to Danny's.

"You're scared. You're terrified."

"I'm scared," Danny said.

"You don't want to die."

Danny looked away from him to the distant lights of the bridge. And as he looked, he knew it was the last time he would ever see them again.

"Only fools die, Danny. Help yourself and live."

The boy slowly turned away from the lights and back to the lean face with the cruel, dead eyes.

"I've come to hate you," he said. "And everything you stand for."

He saw the man stiffen and beyond him the other two become rigid. But he went on speaking, because he couldn't stop the words.

"You died a long time ago. You're a deathman, a deathman, and even she couldn't see it in time."

Collingwood's face had become white, ashen white.

"I know where the painting is. But I'll never tell you. Never."

"You will," Collingwood screamed. "You will."

He struck wildly at him. Danny struggled up and with his last strength grabbed the bloody cane from the man's hands. He then shoved him away hard and faced the other two.

"Come on," he cried, swaying on his feet. "Come on!"

He stood there waiting for them to close in on him, knowing that they would tear his life from him.

"Come on!"

And it was then that he heard the glass doors crash.

"Danny!"

Mr. Warfield's voice. Then other voices filled the room.

"Danny."

He had sunk to his knees again, the cane falling from his grasp. Through a mist he saw the teacher and behind him the gold buttons of uniforms.

"Danny. What did they do to you?"

There were tears on the rugged face.

"Danny."

He knelt at the boy's side and put his arms about him.

"It's all right now," he said. "It's all right."

20

*They were all gone, and only she now remained.
He lay on the bed and looked up at the ceiling, his
eyes half closed. She sat on a chair near him, her
honeyblonde hair glowing in the morning light.*

The nurse popped her head in.

"Visitors all leave?"

"Except one," Danny murmured.

"A special one?"

"Uh-huh."

The nurse laughed and went on down the
corridor. Danny lay back again and rested. The
room was silent and content.

"I was wrong about Mr. Warfield," he said.

"Yes."

"If it weren't for him, I wouldn't be alive
now. It was through him that the police were
able to trace the black limousine to Collingwood's
apartment. He had followed me and had seen me
go into the car and not to the police station. He
knew then that I was in danger."

"You thought he was part of the gang."

"Uh-huh. Warfield did know Cobb from the Army. But he didn't know that Cobb had become a crook. It was Cobb who stole the painting for Collingwood."

"Smitty?"

"He had begun to suspect Cobb. When he saw him talking so long to me explaining the painting, he thought something was wrong — that I was involved somehow. Warfield always went to the museum, so Smitty knew him. He got in touch with him. They both began to watch me. Hoping to get some clue. That's why they were at the rink."

"The note?"

Danny grinned.

"I was wrong about that too."

"Why was Warfield so upset?"

"Because he wrote it while he was very angry. So he put in some pretty tough words about me. Cobb wrote back reminding him of the brutal guard they both had in the Japanese prison camp — telling Warfield not to act like him. It made Warfield ashamed about writing the note. That's why he tore it up into little bits."

He thought of the teacher standing in the room, the note grasped in his scarred hand. But this time it brought no fear to his being.

"The painting is now back at the Brooklyn Museum," she said.

"The true Van Gogh?"

"The true one, Danny."

He smiled at her and reached his hand out. She took it.

"Rest," she said.

He half closed his eyes. And as he did he thought of the woman lying in the snow and the last words she had ever said.

Why are we all so cruel to each other?

He knew that he would spend the rest of his life trying to find the answer to that question.

An answer that would once and for all do away with the question.

His eyes closed and he slept.